IRIS DELANEY would do *anything* to win her father's affection. Would Mac turn on her when her latest scheme went too far?

MAC CORY was blind to Iris's ruthless tricks—until the lives of his wife and child were threatened. What kind of monster had he created with this wayward woman—his own daughter?

RACHEL CORY had left her wicked ways behind . . . yet her newfound innocence made her an easy prey for Iris.

———————————

Series Story Editor **Mary Ann Cooper** is America's foremost soap opera expert. She writes the nationally syndicated column *Speaking of Soaps*, is a major contributor to soap opera magazines, and has appeared on numerous radio and television talk shows.

Author **Dylan Malloy** is a columnist for *Soap Opera Digest* and a script writer for popular daytime soaps. Dylan spends her summers in the hills of Pennsylvania and her winters in Florida with her husband, two Irish Setters, and a tabby cat named Bunny.

From the editor's desk...

Dear Friend,

Captivating . . . delightful . . . heartwarming . . . these are but a few of the enthusiastic comments we've received from Soaps & Serials readers. We're delighted. Every month the fine team of writers and editors at Pioneer pool all their resources to bring you seven new spectacular books.

Based on actual scripts, each novel is written with you in mind. As we recreate the plot and characters of ANOTHER WORLD, we strive to capture the feeling and tone of the show. We can thank our story editor, Mary Ann Cooper, for her sharp attention to details and her genuine love for each and every show.

It's contagious—and we want you to share the spirit! Tell us more about you. How long have you been a fan of ANOTHER WORLD? What other daytime and prime time shows do you watch? How long have you been reading Soaps & Serials?

Keep in touch! And don't miss the special surprise from Mary Ann Cooper in next month's books!

For Soaps & Serials,

Rosalind Noonan

Rosalind Noonan
Editor-in-Chief
Pioneer Communications Network, Inc.

P.S. If you missed previous volumes of ANOTHER WORLD and can't find them in your local book source, please see the order form inserted in this book.

ANOTHER WORLD

9
SUSPICIONS

Soaps™
& Serials

PIONEER COMMUNICATIONS NETWORK, INC.

Suspicions

ANOTHER WORLD paperback novels are published
and distributed by Pioneer Communications Network, Inc.

Copyright © MCMLXXXVI by Procter and Gamble
Productions, Inc.

SOAPS & SERIALS™ is a trademark of Pioneer
Communications Network, Inc.

ISBN: 0-916217-39-6

Printed in Canada

10 9 8 7 6 5 4 3 2 1

SUSPICIONS

Chapter One
New Beginnings

It was a bright, chilly December morning when Pat Randolph arrived in New York City with her new friend and confidant, Dr. David Gilchrist. The flight from Bay City had not been particularly long, but Pat felt as if she'd aged a hundred years as she had sat, rigid and full of misgivings throughout the two-hour ride. Dave had tried to ease her fears, but nothing he said could assuage her. Marianne was Pat's only daughter and she was about to repeat her mother's own tragic, youthful mistake, if she hadn't done so already.

Now in the back seat of a taxi, Pat pulled the mink collar of her fashionable winter-white coat high around her slender neck; even though the cab's heat was on full blast, she couldn't suppress the chill of foreboding that ran up her spine. Dave, tall and boyishly handsome with his shaggy brown hair brushing over his high forehead, attempted to make small talk, commenting on the various sights outside. It was the day after Christmas and the city was dressed up in the glittering finery of the season. Everywhere, there was a feeling of Christmas, from the elaborately decorated store windows along Fifth Avenue to the giant pine tree that dominated Rockefeller Plaza as flushed-faced skaters glided merrily across the ice in the rink below.

It had been the first Christmas that the Randolph family had not spent together. Pat's husband, John, had been both shocked and hurt when he had learned that Marianne had decided to spend the whole Christmas holiday in New York. She would be staying with Glenda Toland, the girlfriend of Michael, Marianne's twin brother. But Pat hadn't been surprised. She could guess why Marianne had departed without a word, leaving Michael to explain. Pat had been through a similar experience herself many years before and she was not about to sit idly by and let it happen to Marianne, too. If she wasn't too late already, that is.

As the cab sped them uptown through the slushy streets to the Toland brownstone, Pat sat quietly, her delicate gloved hands folded tautly in her lap. Halfway through the ride, Dave reached over and put his hand over hers.

"It's going to be all right, Pat," he gently assured her.

She smiled weakly, but something told her it was never going to be all right. *What must John think?* she wondered. Not only had Marianne picked up and left home several days before Christmas, but now Pat had deserted him the day after on the pretext of wanting to keep an eye on their daughter and perhaps catch a couple of after Christmas sales in the bargain. *Pretty feeble excuses,* Pat thought with despair.

"Poor John," she sighed, half aloud. Dave heard her, but only squeezed her hand and said nothing.

Glenda Toland, dressed to go out herself, nearly turned white when she opened the door and saw Pat and Dave. "Mrs. Randolph," she exclaimed, "what are you doing here?"

"Hello, Glenda. I'd like to see Marianne, please," Pat said politely but firmly.

The young woman hesitated, as if trying to pluck an appropriate response out of the thin December air.

"Where is my daughter?" Pat asked more forcefully, her face flushing.

The dark-haired and usually effusive Glenda gulped. "Marianne . . . isn't here, Mrs. Randolph," she stammered, trying desperately to avert Pat's steady gaze.

"Let's have it, Glenda. Where's Marianne?" Dave demanded, growing impatient. "It's important that we speak with her right away."

"Marianne went shopping," she finally blurted out, not at all convincingly. "I was just on my way to meet her," she lied.

Pat eyed her suspiciously. *Something terrible has happened. I can feel it,* she told herself. "I know the real reason Marianne came to New York," Pat heard herself say. "You've got to tell us where she is before it's too late!"

"I told you—"

Pat looked the young woman straight in the eyes. "Do you want to be responsible for Marianne's ruining her life?"

Glenda turned away. "Please, Mrs. Randolph, I gave her my word!"

Feeling desperate, Pat grabbed her roughly by the arm, as if she could pull the truth from her. "I've got to see my daughter. She needs me, much more than you can ever know!" Tears began to well in Pat's cornflower-blue eyes. "Please, Glenda," she whispered, her voice beginning to crack. "Please take me to Marianne!"

Two minutes later, after finally getting the information from Glenda, Pat and Dave were speeding crosstown to the clinic.

"Are you okay?" Dave asked, concerned.

"I'm scared, Dave. Scared to death that I'm too late," she said without looking at him. Her voice had a vacant, empty sound to it, which sent a cold chill through Dave's

9

entire body. If he could have, he would have reached out to her; he would have offered his deep and abiding friendship to sustain her through these agonizing moments of uncertainty. But as he watched her sitting there, so silent and remote, so deep within herself, he knew instinctively that she was beyond receiving whatever comfort he could offer.

Pat's worst fear soon became a reality. When she entered the antiseptic, green room at the end of the long, narrow corridor, she saw Marianne curled on her side in her starched white bed gown, clutching a pillow to her stomach. Although her long chestnut-brown hair covered her face, Pat could tell that her daughter had been crying. For a long moment she stood in the doorway, just watching her little girl. How small, how incredibly vulnerable she looked in that big, forbidding hospital bed. And how horribly out of place this all seemed! It was the day after Christmas. Pat and Marianne should have been back in Bay City with John and Michael. They should have all been gathered around the Christmas tree, singing carols and drinking homemade egg nog. Instead, they were living a nightmare.

Finding her voice, Pat softly called out her daughter's name. The young woman didn't turn, but merely clutched the pillow closer to her, as if clinging to it for dear life. "I'm here, Marianne," Pat whispered as she walked closer to the bed. "I'm not going to leave you, sweetheart."

Marianne turned and propped herself up on one elbow. Her usually bright, brown eyes were indeed red and swollen from crying. Gently sitting on the edge of the bed, Pat could feel her heart breaking as she held her arms open and her little girl immediately leaned into them.

"Oh, Mom," she sobbed. "I'm sorry, Mom. I'm so sorry I disappointed you."

All Pat could do was to smooth her daughter's silky straight hair, soothe her, comfort her, and tell her somehow that they would all get through this, even if Pat herself didn't quite know how.

"I had to do it, Mom," Marianne blurted out as she wiped her teary eyes with the white lace handkerchief Pat had pulled out of her purse. "I really didn't have a choice. Chris didn't love me. How could I take care of a baby all by myself?"

Pat wanted to say she would have helped; that together, the family would have pitched in and made sure the baby had all the love there was to give. But what good would it have done to say any of that? It was Marianne she had to worry about now. Getting her through this ordeal was not going to be easy by any stretch of the imagination. And then there was John. He would have to be told. It was only right.

As if reading her mother's mind, Marianne flew into a panic. "Please, Mom, you can't tell Dad. I would die if he ever found out!"

"How can you even think of keeping something like this from him? You can't continue to lie to him forever, you know. It's just not fair. Your father deserves better than that, don't you think?"

Marianne shook her head violently. She had already suffered the loss of her child, her own flesh and blood; she couldn't risk losing her father's love and respect as well.

"That's not going to happen," Pat promised. "Naturally your father will be disappointed that you didn't confide in him. But he still loves you, sweetheart. He'll understand."

"How can he when I don't even understand myself?" Marianne sobbed pathetically, clutching the pillow against her chest again. "Dad warned me about Chris and I didn't listen. If he knew I was pregnant and had an abortion, he'd never forgive me! I don't know if I can even forgive myself!" she wailed.

The ring of despondency in her daughter's words was like

a knife twisting in Pat's heart. She had never gotten over losing the child she had aborted at Marianne's age. She had always wondered what it would have been like if she had gone through with the pregnancy. It was an emptiness that Pat carried with her every day of her life, one she felt sure Marianne, too, would lock somewhere deep within her heart forever.

"I did the right thing, didn't I, Mom?" The questioning tone in Marianne's voice made Pat quiver inside. She gazed lovingly into her daughter's expectant eyes, but she could not reply. That would have been too dishonest. Tears began to well again in Marianne's eyes. She turned away and pounded her fists into the pillow. "It's not fair. It's just not fair at all. If only Chris had loved me . . . that's all I wanted!" She turned back to her mother. "I really loved him, Mom."

Pat cradled Marianne's head in her arms. After eighteen years, she was still her baby. She always would be. And somehow, some way, Pat would make the pain easier for her daughter to bear.

"I know you did, sweetie. I know you did," she whispered.

When Pat met Dave back in the waiting room, her face was ashen. As a physician, he knew the strain was beginning to take it's toll on her. As a friend, he simply wanted to end her terrible nightmare. That evening, they went to the Plaza. Dave hoped a relaxing dinner might lift her spirits, but Pat barely touched her succulent duck l'orange.

"What am I going to tell John?" she asked at last. "I can't keep on pretending that nothing's wrong. He already suspects something's going on, and I can't lie forever." More likely than not, Pat thought, John would demand an explanation before long and then their already shaky marriage might just split right down the middle.

"I think you're going to have to level with him, Pat," Dave offered.

"But what about Marianne? I promised her I wouldn't tell him, and she'd be devastated if I broke that trust."

"I know Marianne is in pain right now, but she's going to have to take responsibility for her own actions eventually."

"Dave, she just aborted her child!"

"She's also an adult. You can't continue to carry the whole burden for her. It's not fair to either of you."

Pat knew that Dave was right. Marianne was being selfish, expecting her mother to keep her secret. In fact, Marianne often assumed her mother or brother would get her out of whatever mess she got into. But to John, she was always the perfect little princess. Even if Pat were to tell him about the abortion, he'd probably find some way to turn it around and blame her. Still, she couldn't turn her back on her only daughter, especially not now when she knew full well what the poor girl was going through. She desperately hoped that Marianne would decide on her own to confide in her father. But until that time, Pat would have to keep her secret, no matter what the cost.

It was nearly midnight when Dave brought Pat back to her hotel room. After dinner they had walked leisurely down Fifth Avenue. The brisk December night had put a rosy glow in Pat's cheeks and her flaxen, shoulder length hair was slightly tousled by the wind. Gently, Dave smoothed the unruly wisps into place. She gazed into his soulful brown eyes and thought how good it was to have a friend like Dave Gilchrist. How good it was to know that someone else in the world understood her problem and, more amazing than that, actually seemed to care.

"Thank you, Dave. Thank you for everything."

Dave squeezed her hand reassuringly. "If ever I can do anything, please don't hesitate to ask."

Pat smiled gratefully, then went inside and closed the door behind her. Not five seconds later, the phone rang.

"Hello?" Pat answered.

"Mom? I've been calling for hours." Marianne's voice was frantic.

"What's wrong, honey?" Pat asked, suddenly feeling guilty for going out.

"You didn't call Dad, did you?"

"No, Marianne. Dave and I went out for dinner, then for a walk."

Marianne let out a sigh of relief. "Thank goodness! I guess I panicked when I couldn't get you."

"Are you all right, sweetie?" Pat asked gently.

"Yeah, I'll be fine. I just wanted to make sure you hadn't said anything to Dad." Marianne paused. "You won't, will you, Mom?"

"No, of course not. I gave you my word."

"Thanks, Mom. I knew I could count on you!"

"But, Marianne—"

"I'm really tired," she broke in. "I'll see you in the morning, okay?"

"Yes, fine, honey." Pat heard the connection break. For several seconds she continued to hold on to the receiver. Could her own daughter really be so self-absorbed? Could she really care so little about what her mother was going through? Pat felt a tightness in the pit of her stomach. Wearily, she looked at her messages, which she had picked up at the desk before coming up to her room. There were three of them and each one was the same: "Call your husband."

John Randolph stood pensively, gazing out the window of his downtown office. It was a crisp, crystal-clear December morning. The vestiges of the Christmas-night snowfall had remained, framing the streets and sidewalks. John, however, was barely aware of the natural perfection outside. His thoughts were elsewhere; nine hundred miles east in New York City to be exact.

When his son, Michael, had announced that Marianne would be spending the holidays with his girlfriend and her family, his first reaction had been one of absolute disbelief. Christmas had always been a special time in the Randolph house and Marianne's casual treatment of their family tradition disturbed him. What disturbed him even more, though, was Pat's departure for the big city several days after their daughter left. She had told John that she wanted to catch some of the after-Christmas sales in New York. He knew what she really wanted was to check up on Marianne, which was fine with him. He had even offered to accompany her. If the family couldn't all be together for Christmas, John figured at least he and Pat could celebrate with Marianne in New York. But Pat shot down the idea immediately, assuring John that he'd be bored, sitting in a hotel all day long while she and Marianne raided the department stores and boutiques. In the back of his mind, something told him that Pat was just making excuses, that she really didn't want him along at all. Could it be that their marriage, which hadn't exactly been a model of harmony lately, was in serious trouble?

"I just put on a fresh pot of coffee. Want a cup?" Barbara Weaver's distinctive, velvety voice lifted John out of his daydreams.

"Sound's good," he replied without enthusiasm. Barbara smiled and headed for the door. He watched as her tall, slim figure disappeared down the hall and turned left into the kitchenette. It was nice having her for a law partner, he thought with a slight smile, recalling how dead set against going into practice with a woman he'd been at first. But Barbara's gentle persuasiveness, along with her sharp legal mind, had soon made him change his mind. The law seemed to be her whole life. For his part, John was grateful to have Barbara around. Somehow, with her he never had to say very much; she always knew instinctively what was on his mind, just like she had today.

"Okay, what is it this time?" she asked, handing him his mug of coffee.

"You can read me like one of those legal books, can't you?" he teased.

"Better," she countered, taking a sip from her steaming cup. "So, what's wrong? Has Judge Harrison been giving you a hard time again?"

"No, actually he was pretty fair the other day in court."

Barbara's astute gray eyes measured him for a long moment. "Okay, are you going to tell me what's bothering you, or do we both stare at each other like a couple of zombies for the rest of the day?"

No matter how complicated or plain absurd things got, Barbara had a way of cutting through it all and making him smile. Which was exactly what John did, at least for a moment, before his mouth drooped back down into a frown.

"Nothing's that bad, Counselor," she offered.

"It's Pat," he said, sighing heavily. "I don't understand why she's up and left like this. It's not at all like her."

"I didn't think that a little shopping ever hurt anybody," Barbara replied, somewhat guardedly. Had Pat managed to find out the real reason for Marianne's visit to New York? she wondered. A week or two earlier, Barbara had found Marianne on the brink of tears waiting for her father to return from court. Hating to see anyone so upset, she had tried to be her friend by offering a sympathetic ear. Desperately, the young woman blurted out the whole unfortunate business of her pregnancy and possible abortion. It had put Barbara in an awkward position, to say the least, but Marianne obviously needed someone to confide in, and Barbara just happened to be in the right place at the right time.

After hearing the whole horrible story, Barbara had urged Marianne to consider all her options where her family was concerned. But Marianne had refused, maintaining that they would never understand, nor would her father ever forgive her. Barbara listened and advised Marianne as best she could, but she didn't feel it was her place to mention it to John. Now, however, when she looked at him, his brows closely knit and his usually handsome face drawn, she felt absolutely rotten about the whole thing. But then, if Pat did know what was going on, why hadn't she been the one to tell her husband? How could she just let him languish in uncertainty like this? Barbara wondered.

"I don't think I've been paying enough attention to Pat," John said, holding the mug of hot coffee tightly in both his hands. "I've been spending so much time at the office, it's no wonder she's unhappy and bored!"

Barbara wanted to say that if she were Pat Randolph, she'd bend down and kiss the very ground beneath her for her good fortune in finding a man like John. Instead, all she did was pass him the sugar.

An hour later, Barbara came into John's office again. "Alice Frame is waiting outside. Why don't I send her in?" She departed, leaving John to gather his thoughts for a few moments.

It had been over a year since Steven Frame, husband to Pat's younger sister Alice, had died in a plane crash. Alice had tried to fill the gaping emptiness in her life by returning to work as a nurse at Bay City General Hospital. But every night, she had to return to the big, beautiful house Steven had built for her—alone. Only little Sally Spenser's bubbly presence there made coming home worth anything at all. Before Steven died, he and Alice had decided to adopt a child, because Alice was told she could never conceive again. When Sally first came to live with her, it was as if a dark cloud had been lifted from Alice's life. With Steven

17

gone, the adorable little girl was all she had to cling to, and Alice resolved to get the adoption moving along as quickly as possible.

As Alice entered John's office, he thought she seemed a little edgy. He wondered why.

She sat on the sofa and waited to hear the results of John's investigation into Sally's background. It was merely a routine matter, he had assured her, and once all the paper work was done, Sally would be Alice's legal daughter.

"Dad said Pat flew off to New York to do some shopping," Alice said, trying to make conversation to ease her anxiety.

"I don't know what it is about you women and sales," John replied, forcing a small laugh. A brief smile passed across her face as Alice watched closely while he opened a large metal file drawer. He took out a green folder marked SPENSER, SALLY. Slowly, John flipped through several of the pages inside as Alice waited with baited breath.

"There isn't going to be any kind of a problem with the adoption, is there?" she asked, a distinct note of concern in her voice. Alice was well aware that the courts did not approve an adoption for a single parent very often. While everything would have been fine if Steven had still been alive, now that she was widowed, it could put a whole new light on things. Alice brushed back a strand of her long blond hair from her forehead. She could feel small beads of perspiration forming as she watched John's expression grow serious.

"I don't think there will be a problem," he explained guardedly. "It's just that some new information came in late yesterday."

For a moment, Alice felt herself growing faint. She took a deep breath and made tight fists of her hands to burn off the excess adrenaline that was coursing through her body. In an anxious situation like this one, she was glad to have a few medical tricks of the trade up her sleeve, so to speak.

"What exactly did you find out?" she asked as calmly as she could under the circumstances.

"Apparently Sally does have some living relatives. Or at least one anyway," John informed his sister-in-law.

No, this is not happening, Alice told herself. Steven had been ripped out of her life so cruelly, so abruptly, so needlessly. She would not, she *could* not let the same thing happen with Sally.

"Are you sure, John?" Alice asked when she found her voice again.

"I'm afraid so. But," he added quickly, "that's not necessarily going to be a problem."

Deep down, Alice knew that was wishful thinking. "Who are these people? Are they from Bay City?"

"Yes. In fact, one of them is living here right now."

"Do I know them?"

John paused and closed the file. "Yes, you do. Believe it or not, Beatrice Gordon is Sally's grandmother."

Chapter Two
Revelations

Beatrice Gordon was folding the last of Jamie Frame's T-shirts. It seemed like only yesterday that her own son, Raymond, was Jamie's age. Those were the good times, Beatrice thought with a smile. Her beloved daughter, Jennifer, was still with them, and they were a real family. In a way, working as Mac and Rachel Cory's housekeeper was good therapy. It kept Beatrice's mind off of herself and her problems. And more importantly, perhaps, it kept her from being lonely. Between her job at the Corys' and the occasional babysitting she did for Alice Frame's little girl, Sally, Beatrice began to feel that her life was almost complete again. There was also her blossoming friendship with Alice's widowed father, Jim Matthews. All in all, Beatrice felt that things were finally looking up for her.

There were times, however, when she wished Raymond and his family lived closer. But she suspected her son's shrewish wife, Olive, was making sure they remained safely out of reach in California. Olive had done nothing but poison her two young grandsons' minds against their grandmother. By the looks of things, she had done a pretty good job on Raymond, too! Raymond and Beatrice might as well have been on different continents for the amount of time they spent together. Aside from his brief phone calls once or twice a month, they rarely even spoke to each other. But Beatrice was aware that it was not really her son's fault. It was that awful woman he married.

Beatrice was still lost in her own thoughts when the sound of door chimes startled her out of her reverie. Leaving her neatly folded stack of shirts in the laundry room, she hurried down the massive main staircase to the front door. If nothing else, running around from wing to wing in the Cory mansion was certainly helping her to stay in shape.

Alice Frame had the hood of her woolen parka pulled down low over her forehead, and it wasn't until she raised her head that Beatrice recognized her caller.

"Alice, hello, come in! You'll catch your death out there," Beatrice exclaimed.

Alice stepped into the foyer and shook the snow off her coat. The new snowfall had only started about an hour ago, but already the roads were beginning to ice up. Even so, neither wind nor snow could keep Alice from making this visit after her meeting with John Randolph. Her only hope was that she wouldn't have to make small talk with Rachel on top of everything else today. Despite the fact that Alice had seen what a changed woman Rachel was since her marriage to wealthy Mac Cory, it was difficult for her to forget the pain she had caused in her selfish efforts to ruin Alice and Steven's relationship. Perhaps irrationally, Alice often thought that she and Steven could have had so much more precious time together if it hadn't been for Rachel's meddling.

But, standing in the foyer of the Cory mansion where Rachel was now enjoying a full and carefree life, Alice couldn't help be happy for the once-troubled woman. Rachel had acted out of desperation, unable to let go of someone she loved. Right now Alice was experiencing the same emotions toward Sally. In fact, it was her love and concern for her young ward that prompted the unexpected visit.

"Mr. and Mrs. Cory are out until this evening," Beatrice informed Alice as she entered the spacious living room with its high, vaulted ceilings and Oriental carpeted floors.

Where do I begin? Alice asked herself as she looked into Beatrice's face with searching eyes. "Actually . . . I've come to see . . . you, Beatrice," she said haltingly.

"Did you want me to sit for Sally tonight?"

"No, but it is about Sally." Alice could see the concern in Beatrice's eyes. There was not a doubt in her mind that the older woman cared deeply for the child. They had formed the kind of bond of friendship that young children and older people often do. But then again, it was easy to fall completely in love with Sally Spenser. The way her curious blue eyes sparkled when she spoke, the way she bubbled over with excitement and enthusiasm for life was all part of what made the little girl so unique.

As Alice stood facing Beatrice, she suddenly realized the full scope of her love for her foster child. She hoped that Beatrice could see the depth of this love, too. But if she didn't, Alice was prepared to fight like a fury to keep her child with her.

"Nothing's wrong with Sally, is there?" Beatrice asked, her voice filled with genuine concern.

"No, no," Alice assured her. "She's fine. In fact, she's at a Brownie troop meeting at Suzy Mitchell's house around the corner."

Beatrice seemed to relax somewhat. She poured Alice a cup of hot tea and then looked at her. "You said you came about Sally?"

"Yes," Alice said slowly. "As you know, I'm trying to adopt her. It was something Steve and I had planned to do before he died."

"You'll make a wonderful mother, dear. It's such a shame your husband can't be with you so the three of you could be a real family."

Yes, Alice thought bittersweetly. First she had lost their baby, then she had been told by the doctors that she could never have another one. Then Steven had been taken from her. When Sally came to live with her, things had started to look up for the first time in a long time. Alice had long since learned not to dwell on the past. Now it was time to begin a new life and, thank God, she had Sally to share it with—or at least, she'd thought she had Sally: until this morning.

"I've had John Randolph look into Sally's hospital records," Alice began slowly. "It's fairly routine before going ahead with an adoption."

"But I thought Sally's parents were both dead?" Beatrice questioned.

"They are, but John managed to locate another family member." Alice could feel the blood rushing to her pale cheeks. For hours after speaking to John, she had toyed with the idea of keeping the truth to herself and trying to slide the adoption through without anyone being the wiser. But in all fairness, she couldn't. Both Sally and Beatrice had a right to know the truth. They were family and family was too precious to be ignored. As she looked into Beatrice's confused gray eyes, Alice also realized that once this woman knew who Sally really was, she was going to have an uphill battle on her hands. Bracing herself, Alice took a sip of hot tea. It felt warm and calming inside her, and for a moment it made her whole body feel safe and protected by its intoxicating heat.

"You mean Sally isn't an orphan?" Beatrice asked, surprised.

"No, she has a grandmother," Alice said quickly, averting Beatrice's steady gaze.

"A grandmother? How wonderful!" Beatrice exclaimed, forgetting herself for a moment. Then she quickly went on, "Oh, dear, that could make things difficult for you, couldn't it."

If Alice didn't realize it before, she was certainly convinced of just how difficult the adoption could be by the tone in Beatrice's voice.

"Have you met this woman?" she asked.

Alice swallowed hard. "Beatrice, I don't know how to tell you this. . . ."

"What is it, Alice?"

"*You* are Sally's grandmother."

It took the rest of the afternoon and half of the evening for Beatrice to get over the shock of Alice's announcement. All she could think was that she had been given a second chance. Where she had failed with Jenny, she would succeed with Jenny's daughter, Sally. For the first time in a very long time, Beatrice actually allowed herself to look toward the future with anticipation. The only stumbling block was Alice Frame. She didn't know exactly how, but Beatrice knew she would have to deal with Alice—and soon. Beatrice could barely remember what she had said to her or how, or even when, she had left the Cory house. She was so caught up in this new world unraveling before her that she couldn't focus on anything else. Moreover, she was determined to do things right this time. Sally was family and families should stay together, no matter what. She had learned that a long time ago—the hard way.

Rachel Cory was in total agreement with her housekeeper. Knowing how important her own family was during her childhood, Rachel encouraged Beatrice to take action. But having been a passive person for most of her life, Beatrice was somewhat unsure of how to proceed. Although she knew she wanted her granddaughter, she hadn't the vaguest idea of what she was supposed to do. Unable to keep from trying to help, Rachel wrote a number on a slip of paper and handed it to her housekeeper.

"Who is Scott Bradley?" Beatrice asked, staring at the name.

"A lawyer. He's a friend of Mac's and mine," Rachel explained.

"Why should I call a lawyer?"

Rachel could see that Beatrice's resolve was beginning to crumble, but she was determined to help the woman in spite of herself. Rachel couldn't help but think of her son and the child she was carrying; if something ever happened to her and Mac, God forbid, she would want her mother to assume the responsibility of her children. "Sally is your own flesh and blood," Rachel exclaimed. "She's your daughter's child, Beatrice. Surely you want to adopt her yourself?"

The reality of this possibility had not actually occurred to Beatrice. "But I'm her grandmother. Why should I have to adopt her?"

"Because she's been a ward of the court since she was born. Legally, Sally's an orphan. If you want custody of her, you're going to have to start proceedings immediately."

"You mean I'd have to fight Alice in court?"

The impact of her words hit Rachel full force. She hadn't even considered Alice's feelings, she was so concerned with Beatrice and Sally. But she still felt that even if Alice was hurt, the pain would be temporary compared to the anguish Beatrice would have for the rest of her life. "I know it doesn't seem fair to Alice, and it won't be easy, but if you want Sally, that's what you're going to have to do," Rachel explained softly.

"Of course I want her, but . . ." Beatrice hesitated.

"Then call Scott Bradley. Sally has already lost both her parents. Do you want her to lose her grandmother, too?"

Rachel's words jolted Beatrice, but not enough to make her want to pick up the phone. Yes, she wanted Sally. Yes, she loved her. But so did Alice.

"Sally is your flesh and blood," Rachel repeated, this time more gently. "She needs you. And whether you admit or not, you need her."

When Iris Delaney arrived at the Cory house, she learned that Rachel was in the new studio Mac had built for her in the west wing, busily working on a clay sculpture. Lately, Iris had been making it a point to drop in at her father's house unexpectedly, hoping to catch Rachel doing something amiss so she could hurry back and report the *faux pas* to Mac. Today she got more than she'd bargained for when Jamie let it slip that his mother was helping Beatrice try to win custody of Sally from Alice.

"And how is your mother going to do that?" Iris asked, tousling the boy's fine, light brown hair.

"She told Mrs. Gordon to call Mr. Bradley," Jamie replied, finishing his glass of milk.

Iris smiled with satisfaction. *So Rachel is meddling in Alice's life again. Daddy isn't going to like that one little bit.*

"You want me to tell Mom you're here?" Jamie asked innocently.

"No, dear, I'll see her later. In fact, you don't even have to tell her I came over."

Not one to ever put off doing anything, Iris swung into action immediately. On the pretext of wanting to get her husband and Scott Bradley together for a long overdue social evening, Iris called Scott and invited him over to dinner. When she wanted to, Iris could charm the spots off a leopard with her beguiling, feline smile and subliminal air of sensuality. Her petite, well-endowed body was always perfumed from head to toe with the most intoxicating, most expensive scent known to man. For Iris Cory Carrington Delaney, nothing less would have sufficed.

Taken in by her considerable charms himself, Robert was more than a little disconcerted that evening as he stood by and watched his wife work her wiles on the unsuspecting Scott Bradley.

"I hope Daddy is treating you well," she said, her baby-blue eyes twinkling with mischief as she smiled at her guest.

"I couldn't ask for anything better than to work for Mac Cory," Scott replied with complete honesty. After all, it isn't every day that a bright, young lawyer gets the opportunity to head the legal department of a prestigious company like Cory Publishing. Though a part of him longed to branch out on his own and start his own firm, much like John Randolph had done, the other part of Scott was very satisfied with the creature comforts that his job at Cory provided. Still, he did take on an independent case or two from time to time.

"Scott, I'm sure this is nothing but silly gossip, but I heard you were giving Beatrice Gordon legal advice," Iris pried in her most innocent voice.

"For heaven's sake, Iris, Scott's business with his clients is confidential. You know that!" Robert snapped.

Iris continued to look directly at Scott, not the least bit dissuaded. "I'm sure Scott knows I would never ask him to divulge privileged information about a client. I only mentioned that I'd heard that nasty rumor."

Scott smiled awkwardly, meeting Iris's steady gaze. "As a matter of fact, Beatrice is a client. That's hardly a secret, though."

"Oh, Scott. I'm so sorry to hear that!" Iris sighed mournfully. She could almost predict his reaction.

"Why shouldn't Beatrice Gordon have legal advice if she wants it?"

"Don't mind Iris," Robert interrupted, shooting a warning look at his wife.

"Robert, I think Scott has a right to know the facts," she insisted.

"What facts?" Scott asked, genuinely perplexed.

"The fact is, Iris, you're sticking your nose where it doesn't belong. Now let's just drop it and take our brandys inside," Robert said firmly.

But Iris wasn't about to be silenced, especially not by the likes of Robert Delaney, who couldn't even run his own life. How dare he think he could run hers. He hadn't even enough self-control to keep from bedding down with his frowsy little waitress friend and getting her pregnant. She'd had to rescue him from that dreadful situation by marrying him herself. No, Robert was no match for Iris. Mac Cory was the only man on her life who could level Iris with so much as a glance much less a word. Robert could never fill her father's shoes, Iris thought smugly.

"Well, I for one do not intend to sit back and allow Scott to proceed blindly and be the instrument of destruction for two innocent human beings!" she cried, her voice filled with righteous indignation.

"What are you talking about, Iris?" Scott asked, now more intrigued than anything else.

"Why Alice Frame, of course. You can't just help Beatrice Gordon destroy her life!"

"Believe me, I have no intention of destroying anyone's life," Scott replied, somewhat defensively.

"Do you realize how long Alice has been waiting to adopt Sally?" Iris challenged.

"Drop it, Iris," Robert hissed.

Iris glared at her husband with disdain, then turned her attention back to Scott. "No one could love that little girl more than Alice. If you help Beatrice Gordon separate them, you'll be helping to destroy not one, but two lives. Do you really want that on your conscience, Scott?"

Robert slammed his brandy glass down on the table. "That's it," he said, rising angrily from his chair. "I apologize for my wife's interference, Scott. But as you can see, she has a mind of her own. And to my knowledge, she has never once listened to anyone's reasoning but her own, however twisted it may be."

Snatching up the bottle of brandy, Robert stalked out of the dining room, slamming the door shut behind him. Scott turned toward Iris; looking a bit embarrassed. She, on the other hand, was not even the slightest bit ruffled.

"You'll have to forgive Robert's bad manners. He's been going through a difficult time professionally."

"I think it's time I left anyway," Scott replied, heading for the door.

Iris helped him with his coat. "All I ask is that you consider what I've said. After all, Beatrice probably would have never even made an issue of any of this if Rachel hadn't egged her on."

"What's Rachel got to do with it?" Scott asked.

"Why, Scott, I thought you knew. Rachel hates Alice. She always has." Scott fixed her with a skeptical look. "Oh, I know Rachel's made a big pretext of being Alice's friend, but that's all it is, a pretext. Deep down she's still the same scheming, jealous woman, out to punish Alice for taking Steve away from her." Iris paused. "Scott, can't you see that Sally's the only one who's going to suffer here. Is that what you really want?" Iris's eyes were beginning to well with carefully rehearsed crocodile tears.

After Scott left, Iris smiled at her reflection in the hall mirror. She felt sure she had squelched Rachel's attempt to manipulate the situation with Sally. Now all she had to do was let Mac know about his wife's interference in Alice's life. *Daddy will not like that one little bit*, she told her reflection silently.

"I guess you're pretty happy with yourself?" Robert's accusatory voice sounded from behind her.

Iris turned and held his gaze for a long moment, then yawned to show her disdain. "I'm going to bed," she

announced and started up the hand-carved marble staircase.

"I'm not finished with you!" Robert yelled after her.

Iris continued to mount the stairs. *Well, I'm certainly
finished with you. At least for tonight,* she thought to herself,
smiling inwardly. The evening had been a brilliant success!

In the Randolph kitchen, John was standing over the stove,
waiting for the tea kettle to whistle. Whenever he did that,
Pat would tease him. "A watched pot never boils," she'd
say, laughing. Tonight, however, John was all alone in the
big empty house and he really didn't care if he stood there
all night long. At least it was something to do. At least it
might keep his thoughts from drifting to Pat and Marianne,
who were still somewhere in New York, he supposed.

He had just put a tea bag in his mug when he heard the
front door open. Maybe Michael had decided not to go to
the movies after all and had come over to keep the old man
company, he told himself. Secretly, he hoped that was the
case.

"A watched pot never boils," came Pat's soft voice from
the entrance. John spun around, his dark eyes lighting up
immediately.

"Pat! I don't believe it! Why didn't you call? I would
have picked you up at the airport."

She smiled nervously. "We wanted to surprise you," she
lied. In fact, Dave Gilchrist had offered to drive her and
Marianne home, but Pat had insisted he just call them a
cab. It was going to be difficult enough to face John, and
the last thing Pat needed was to run the risk that he would
somehow find out that Dave had been with her. How would
she ever have been able to explain that away?

"You mean Marianne's home, too?" John asked, bubbling over with happiness. Pat couldn't bear to see her
husband's joy. *If he only knew the truth,* she told herself. But

for Marianne's sake, Pat would have to steel herself and cover for her daughter as best she could. Yet as she looked into John's ecstatic face, Pat knew it would be the hardest thing she'd ever had to do. She knew too, that keeping a secret like this one could be fatal to a marriage. But she really didn't have much choice in the matter.

"Marianne went right upstairs to unpack," Pat smiled stiffly as John hugged her warmly.

"I guess my two girls did a number on those Fifth Avenue shops, huh?"

"We sure gave it the old college try," she replied with practiced animation.

"I really missed you, Pat," John said softly. "Except for the few times Michael came to visit, this house has been like a tomb."

"I missed you, too," she said, hoping to reassure him. But in all honesty, she was trying to convince herself more than John. The truth of it was that she really hadn't given him much thought at all, except to wonder how she would be able to deal with this very moment when it finally arrived. *And I'm not dealing very well at all,* she thought as John kissed her tenderly. Pat tried to respond, but her husband immediately sensed that something was wrong.

"What is it, Pat?"

"Nothing," she lied. "I guess I'm just tired from the flight. You know . . ."

John hugged her lovingly. "I guess I'm not a very considerate husband, am I? Why don't I fix us some tea and then we'll tuck you right in bed, young lady!"

Pat smiled, grateful for the reprieve. She could tell that John's kisses, so hot and eager on her icy lips, begged for a warm response. But it was no use. It was as if a part of her had ceased to exist. There was no sensation, no longing, only the urgent desire to be left alone in her own private world where, cold and untouchable, she could be the guardian of the terrible secret. As they left the kitchen arm in arm, Pat heard the tea kettle begin to whistle.

"Hot tea would be very nice. Thank you, John."

Marianne was the last one down for breakfast the next morning. She handed John a beautifully wrapped box from Bloomingdale's. "Merry Christmas, Daddy," she said giving him a quick hug. Pat watched John as his fingers ripped through the shiny red paper. His whole face lit up like a Christmas tree when he held up the camel-colored cardigan sweater.

"It's real cashmere," Marianne announced.

"It's beautiful, sweetheart," he said as she helped him put it on.

"I thought you'd look really classy in this at the office. Wait till Barbara gets a load of you."

At the mention of Barbara Weaver's name, Pat felt her face harden. Perhaps she was just a little jealous that John's law partner seemed to be privy to all the family's personal business. Or perhaps . . . But Pat quickly dismissed it. Barbara had been a good friend to the Randolph family. She was John's trusted and admired right hand and that was that. Anything else was plain foolishness.

"Wait'll I get the bill," John teased as he modeled his gift.

"I paid for that out of my own allowance!" Marianne retorted.

"That's what they always say," her father said, smiling broadly.

Pat watched her husband and daughter with a detached sense of wonderment. Anyone would think that everything was perfectly normal, that here was your average happy American family enjoying breakfast together, interacting, laughing as though they hadn't a care in the world. It was incredible.

32

Pat wished with all her heart that she could join in and be a part of this happy gathering. But that was just the problem. She was physically there, all right. She was serving up their pancakes and poached eggs, squeezing the orange juice and pouring the coffee. But she was not there emotionally, not really, not enough that it added to the family atmosphere. Families shared things. Families did not keep secrets.

That evening, Michael picked Marianne up to preregister for winter classes at Bay State. Marianne, determined to get her life back in gear, had decided to begin college. Her father had been very disappointed when she had not registered for the past September's classes, and she was through disappointing her father.

John suggested that he and Pat have dinner out, and eager for the opportunity to get out of the house, Pat agreed. The evening was pleasant enough, especially since she was away from all the reminders of what she'd been through. Pat was actually able to sit back and relax in the elegant atmosphere of Tall Boys. She even encouraged John to linger over an after-dinner brandy while they listened to the piano music in the lounge. All Pat cared about was postponing the inevitable return home, where everything would start to close in on her all over again.

It was almost midnight when John turned the key in the front door. He smiled to himself as he and his wife went up the stairs to check on Marianne before going to their own room. He had longed for this moment for days. Ever since Pat had left for New York, all he could think about was holding her in his arms and making love to her. Once in their bedroom, John waited patiently in bed for his wife to come out of the bathroom.

Pat, however, was in no hurry. She looked at her pale, makeupless face in the medicine chest mirror. Ever since that moment in the hospital room, she had been dreading this moment. She brushed her hair fifty strokes . . . one hundred . . . one hundred and fifty, hoping that by the time she went inside, John would be asleep. He wasn't.

As she slid under the covers, Pat felt her husband's warm body press against hers.

"I've missed you so much," he whispered, brushing her hair off her forehead. His mouth fell to her neck and his hands urgently caressed her. Pat lay there, stiff as a corpse, her eyes shut tight, as if that could block out everything else. John stopped and propped himself up on his elbow. He gazed down at her, hurt, confused, and filled with unsatisfied desire.

"What's wrong, Pat?"

She opened her eyes slowly. "It must have been all the wine. I'm really tired, John." With that, she rolled over on her side. She held her breath, counting the seconds until John finally rolled over on his side, too, snapping the covers over his chest as he breathed out a long, frustrated sigh.

He was even more troubled the next morning when he saw a note in Pat's handwriting on the pad beside the phone. "Dave Gilchrist—1:00."

Chapter Three
Strained Relations

There was a deafening silence around the breakfast table at the Randolph house on Monday morning. It had not been the best of weekends to say the least. Pat had avoided her husband like the plague, and Marianne had inadvertantly done the same. Understandably, John was put out and downright angry that he had been made to feel like a stranger in his own home. Every time he'd tried to ask Marianne about her trip to New York, she would find some excuse to change the subject. But Marianne was a teenager and a certain amount of moodiness was to be expected. Pat, however, was another story entirely. All weekend he had tried to approach her, not to make love, but just to talk husband to wife. It was no use. She would close up and withdraw, and John wanted to know why.

"More coffee, John?" Pat asked politely. Marianne had made a quick exit some moments before, obviously uncomfortable because of the tension between her parents, John was sure.

"I'd like to know what's going on around here?"

"What do you mean?" Pat asked, holding her breath.

"I know something's wrong," John insisted.

"Like what?" she asked, forcing a smile.

"If I knew that, I wouldn't be asking!" He fixed her with a long, appraising look. "All I know is you've changed." When this outburst didn't merit a response, he slammed his hand against the table. Throwing the morning paper aside, he got up and stormed out of the room.

"Oh, Marianne," Pat whispered, "we can't go on like this. *I* can't go on!"

At the office, Barbara couldn't help but notice her partner's downtrodden spirits. From the moment she first interviewed to work in John's firm, Barbara had felt a deep admiration for her boss, which had grown in the months that followed. He was the most fair and compassionate man she had ever known. A brilliant lawyer and a formidable opponent, John was respected by his collegues without reservation. Any of the attorneys in Bay City's prosecution department would have attested to that. Often, Barbara would stay late in the office, just to read some of the cases he had prepared. More than anything, she wanted John's admiration and to be invaluable to him in all things. Thus, when he invited her to be his partner, it was the highest form of flattery. That he would consider her his equal was more than she'd dared to hope.

But even though Barbara was still somewhat awed by John, their relationship had begun to grow into a deep and trusting friendship. They worked well together. In fact, one could say they complemented each other. Her wry humor could undercut his most serious moods, and he could cut her down to size with a simple look. In short, they were comfortable together. Barbara had also become like a member of the family, dining at their home often. Michael and Marianne had always received her warmly, treating her more as a peer than as their father's friend. Pat was cordial, though not openly solicitous of her friendship. That, of course, did not surprise Barbara one bit. If the situation were reversed, she'd feel exactly the same way. Although she did not consciously envy Pat, every once in a while Barbara would catch herself frowning inwardly when John happened to mention his wife's name. Perhaps deep down she didn't really believe that Pat, with her somewhat patrician aloofness, appreciated what a fine man she had. John, on the other hand, seemed to always be bending over backwards for his wife, which was precisely why it hurt Barbara to see him so distressed.

"Maybe I haven't been spending enough time with Pat," he offered lamely.

Barbara had to bite her tongue. True, John often had to work late, but he more than made up for it. He devoted every single weekend to his family and his darling Pat. What more could a woman want?

"Have you told Pat how you feel, John?" Barbara asked, chiefly out of concern for his feelings, which seemed pretty raw at the moment.

"She doesn't seem to want to hear anything I have to say. I think Pat's tuned me out, Barbara."

"Then you've got to try again and keep trying until she listens," Barbara counseled.

John shook his head. "I don't know. Maybe it goes deeper than I'm willing to admit. Maybe there's something fundamentally wrong with our marriage."

Barbara laid her slender hand on John's arm. "You love Pat, and I'm sure she loves you, too. Whatever's wrong, you can get through it. Just be patient. Maybe Pat's going through some kind of an emotional crisis. We women are pretty funny that way, you know."

For the first time all day, John actually smiled. As far as Barbara was concerned, that alone made all her efforts worth while.

"I don't know what I'd do without you to cheer me up. You're a real lifesaver, Barbara," John said gratefully.

Barbara just smiled.

That afternoon, Liz Matthews went over to the Randolph house to invite her niece's family for New Year's dinner. Pat, however, had left earlier to keep an appointment with Dave Gilchrist at Bay City General Hospital.

"I hope your mother isn't letting herself get run down again," Liz remarked to Marianne, who was sprawled out on the parlor couch reading.

"There's nothing wrong with Mom, Aunt Liz," she replied curtly.

Liz raised her eyebrows. "Well, I see I caught you in a good mood."

Marianne slammed her book closed. "Just don't bug me, okay?"

"Are you going to tell me what's wrong?" Liz persisted.

"Nothing is wrong! We're all just fine." She stomped out of the room and raced up the stairs to her bedroom, slamming the door behind her. Liz shook her head. Poor Marianne was such a sensitive child, she thought. No doubt she was upset about Pat, Liz reasoned. There was obviously something Pat Randolph wasn't telling her aunt. In fact, Liz had recently mentioned to her brother-in-law, Jim Matthews, that Pat had not seemed quite like herself for weeks. As usual, Jim denied his daughter was having any kind of a problem and then told Liz in no uncertain terms to keep her nose out of Pat's affairs.

Why none of them could understand that she was only concerned with their welfare was beyond Liz. Whenever anything was going on, the whole family would just shut her out. But Liz was determined to help them despite the hostility she got in return. One look at Marianne told her the whole story. There was trouble in the Randolph house and Liz was determined to get to the bottom of it.

Later that day, Liz met Iris Delaney for lunch at Tall Boys. Liz had always admired Iris's sense of style and the air of authority with which she was able to order her world. That, plus the fact that she was Mac Cory's daughter, was an irresistible combination. Iris had also often said that she wished Mac would come to his senses about Rachel and start looking for someone with proper breeding—someone like Liz Matthews. Liz had been quite flattered and since then never missed an opportunity to socialize with Mac's beautiful and so obviously well-informed daughter whenever the occasion presented itself.

As the women sipped their martinis, Liz was not her usual, talkative self.

"What's wrong, Liz? You seem troubled," she asked with a sweetness that passed for genuine concern.

Liz put down her drink and let out a long, frustrated sigh. "I'm afraid my niece, Pat, may not be well."

"It's nothing serious, I hope?" Iris asked, probing for more information.

"I'm not really sure. No one will tell me anything. I tried to talk to Marianne, but she clammed right up on me."

"What makes you think Pat is ill?" Iris inquired.

"Well, for one thing, she had an appointment with Dave Gilchrist over at the hospital today."

"It's probably just a routine checkup," Iris offered, seeming to dismiss Liz's concern. Her inquisitive gaze surveyed the lavishly appointed room, and just happened to light on a table for two, discreetly tucked away in a corner. She smiled to herself.

"Liz, isn't that John sitting over in the corner?" she asked, feigning innocence.

Liz put on her glasses. Immediately, she felt her heart sink. No wonder Marianne was walking around the house wearing a frown that practically touched the floor. *Poor Pat*, Liz bemoaned, *John is at it again!*

"Isn't that Barbara Weaver sitting with him?" Iris pressed.

"It certainly is!" Liz exclaimed, not even trying to hide her displeasure. From the moment that woman had set her foot in John's office, Liz had warned Pat that she would be trouble. "It's a case of history repeating itself," she had reminded her niece. But Pat wouldn't hear of it. She assured her aunt that what had happened between John and Steve Frame's assistant, Bernice Kline, was over and done with. It would never happen again. But Liz knew better. Men like John Randolph were vulnerable to the designs and manipulations of ambitious women like Bernice Kline —and Barbara Weaver. Why, Barbara had barely been in John's office for a few months before he made her a full partner. Surely that was proof enough of the man's lack of judgment.

Pat, however, disagreed. She argued that her husband was overworked and that Barbara was the perfect solution, someone to share his responsibility. Liz, however, was quite sure that Barbara had every intention of sharing a great deal more than that. And now, Pat was feeling ill again, just like before. She had nearly ruined her health once with all the drinking. John's affair with Bernice had driven her to that. And now, by all indications, it was starting up again and with the same type of a woman. Barbara was ambitious, to be sure. She certainly was not going to remain content to be John's partner in business alone. She was clearly staking her claim for more . . . much more.

"Oh well, it's probably only a business lunch," Iris suggested in a tone that made it very clear she meant just the opposite.

"They certainly look cozy," Liz muttered.

"Oh, Liz, you don't think . . . you aren't suggesting that anything is going on between John and Barbara?"

Liz gritted her teeth as she shot the couple a menacing look. That was exactly what she was suggesting!

"I wouldn't put it past John," she replied in a cold voice. "After all, he's done that sort of thing before!"

"Really?" Iris asked, hanging on her friend's every word.

Ordinarily, Liz would have divulged the whole, ugly story about John and Bernice, but this time she caught herself. She couldn't hurt her darling Pat by telling Iris about her troubled past.

"Men and their roving eyes," Liz said, trying to cover.

Iris would probably have probed further if Scott Bradley hadn't just then approached their table to say hello.

"I wanted to thank you for dinner the other night," he said to Iris. She turned on her usual charm, and smiled engagingly.

"Won't you join us for a drink?" she asked.

"I'd really like to, but I have to meet a client," he apologized.

Iris's face turned up into a little girl pout. "I do hope you've given some thought to what we talked about?"

Scott smiled politely and then glanced at his watch. "I've really got to run," he said, evading her. "Nice seeing you, Iris, Liz."

Iris arched her brow quizzically as she followed his figure out of the room with her eyes.

"What was that all about?" Liz asked, her curiosity sorely tempted.

"Well, I'm not sure I should mention this . . ." Iris began, leading Liz on.

"Iris, you know you can tell me anything. It won't go any farther than this table."

"Actually, it does concern you," Iris went on.

"Then you've got to tell me, dear. What's going on?"

"It's about Beatrice Gordon," Iris replied, watching Liz for a reaction.

Liz set her jaw in anger. Beatrice Gordon was a self-seeking, manipulative woman if she'd ever seen one, Liz thought. She was a nobody and yet, in a short time, she had managed to worm her way into Jim Matthews's affections. Obviously, she did not want to spend the rest of her life as the Corys' housekeeper.

Liz was painfully aware that Jim had been lonely since his wife, Mary, had passed on. For her part, Liz had been more than willing to offer comfort and support. She even thought Jim was starting to like her just a little. Then Beatrice Gordon had come along with those soulful eyes and upset the whole applecart! Jim was behaving like a lovesick schoolboy chasing after that woman, who was obviously just trying to spur his interest by playing hard to get.

And to Liz's amazement, it was working. Jim had asked Beatrice out to dinner several times, and even gotten all spiffed up to boot. He had never once done that for her, Liz reflected glumly. How easy it was to pull the wool over some men's eyes, she observed. Opportunists like Beatrice Gordon made it impossible for decent women like herself to breathe the same air.

"What about Beatrice Gordon?" Liz finally asked her companion.

Iris laid her hand consolingly over Liz's hand. "I wish I wasn't the one who had to tell you this, dear, but Beatrice is trying to take Sally away from Alice!"

It was Beatrice's afternoon off, and she was glad for the opportunity to spend it with her friend, Ada McGowen. Ada's kitchen, with it's old-fashioned stove and ice-box refrigerator gave Beatrice a feeling of security. She sensed that she belonged there rather than in the state-of-the-art Cory kitchen with all its new-fangled gadgets and modern appliances.

Ada poured them coffee from her twenty-year-old percolator coffee pot and put out a plate of homemade sugar doughnuts, which were still hot from the oven.

"You sounded pretty upset over the phone," Ada noted. "Want to tell me why?"

"Why do you say that?" Beatrice asked. "Nothing's wrong."

"You must be upset," Ada decided, ignoring her friend's question. "You've been sitting here for five minutes and you haven't even tasted this batch of doughnuts," she teased, trying to break the ice.

Beatrice smiled wearily. "There's no fooling you is there, Ada?"

"Okay, Bea, what gives? Has Liz Matthews been driving you up the wall about Jim again?"

"No, nothing like that," Beatrice told her friend. "It's about Sally Spenser, Ada."

"What about her?"

Beatrice raised her head and looked Ada straight in the eyes. "She's my granddaughter."

It wasn't quite that Beatrice didn't know her own mind, she did. She also knew her heart. And both were telling her to fight for her granddaughter. But there were other considerations. Alice Frame, whom she admired and respected, was one. Sally had grown to love and depend on Alice, that was plain enough. *Do I really have the right to come in and take the child away from her simply because I'm her natural grandmother*, Beatrice asked herself. Was it even realistic for a woman of her years to consider taking on the care and responsibility of such a young and impressionable child? But above and beyond all of that, there was one, unchangeable fact: Sally was her own flesh and blood. In her heart, Beatrice knew that Rachel Cory was right. Blood belonged with blood. Ada McGowen didn't agree.

"You're going to hurt that little girl if you drag her through a custody fight. I can't believe you really want to do that, Bea."

"What choice have I got if Alice won't drop the adoption petition?" Beatrice asked, the strain showing.

"Are you nuts, Bea?" Ada asked in her typically no-nonsense way. "Sally belongs with Alice and I can't believe you honestly don't know that. You're her grandmother, so be her grandmother. Let Alice do the mothering."

Something within Beatrice rebelled at that thought. Why should her own flesh and blood grow up in a stranger's home, knowing nothing of her own, natural family? It was true, of course, that Beatrice had no real home of her own at the moment, but she did have her late husband's small pension. But could she support Sally on that alone? she wondered. Then there was Sally's schooling to think of. How could Beatrice possibly manage to put her through college? All at once, Beatrice could feel her head start to spin. It was all so mind-boggling. Yet, she had a stubborn streak that unequivocally resisted the option to sit back, do nothing and be content with whatever type of arrangement Alice Frame allowed her. Rachel was right, Beatrice told Ada. A child belonged with its family.

"Sometimes Rachel ought to mind her own business," Ada snapped, sounding annoyed that her daughter was involving herself in Alice's affairs again. But Beatrice assured Ada that Rachel had not been meddling.

"All Rachel did was tell me about her father and how deeply she regretted not having him around when she was growing up."

"Gerald Davis was nothing but a bum!" Ada quipped. "Rachel has this fairy-tale idea about the kind of father he was, but she knows good and well that the guy couldn't care less about her." Ada laughed at Rachel's naiveté. "When she finally found her father after all those years, the only thing he was interested in was whether or not she could provide the cash to set him up in business. So much for paternal devotion!" But Beatrice knew what really worried Ada was the thought that her daughter's old sense of competition with Alice might be starting to surface again. Although Rachel had certainly turned over a new leaf since her marriage to Mac, and had supposedly buried the hatchet with Alice, vestiges of their old rivalry could still pop up every once in a while, and this definitely seemed to be one of those times.

"I want you to forget what Rachel told you," Ada counseled Beatrice. "You've got to think this thing through on your own."

"I'm doing that, Ada," Beatrice replied defensively.

"Then don't do something you're going to regret later. You and Sally can still have a great relationship if Alice adopts her. Don't invite a lot of bitterness by putting Sally in the middle with you and Alice pulling at opposite ends. Nobody's going to win anything that way." She paused and added in a softer tone, "Just think on it, okay?"

Beatrice promised she would. But in her heart, she had already made her decision.

Not long after Beatrice left Ada's, Rachel opened the door and found her mother waiting impatiently to talk to her. Understandably, Rachel was both hurt and angry at her mother's attitude.

"I can't believe you think I'd try to hurt Alice," Rachel gasped, her hazel eyes wide with affrontry. "You know how hard I've tried to make up for the pain I caused her."

"You had no right to interfere with Alice's adopting Sally and you know it!" Ada maintained.

"Please, Ma, you're wrong. Just let me explain—"

"Did you or did you not advise Beatrice to fight Alice's custody petition?" Ada interrupted.

"She has a right to have custody of her own grandchild," Rachel protested, her eyes flashing with indignation. "Ma, they're family!"

"That's not the issue and you know it!" Ada flared back.

Rachel felt the blood flooding to her cheeks. Her mother was being inflexible and refusing to see any side but Alice's. And worse than that, she obviously believed that Rachel was up to her old schemes again. "Can't you understand this has nothing to do with Alice?"

"It has nothing to do with you either!" Ada insisted. She took a deep breath and went on, "Look, you've got a loving husband. Soon the two of you will have a new baby. Why can't you just count your blessings and leave everybody else alone?"

Rachel hadn't seen her mother so angry in a long time and suddenly she felt irrationally angry at Alice for making Ada take sides again. All through those long years that Rachel had been so in love with Steve Frame, Ada had never once defended her. It was always poor, mistreated Alice who got Ada's sympathy, while all Rachel got was rebuke. Even though she knew now that her mother had been right all along, the rejection still hurt. Rachel turned away from her mother. "I'm sorry if you don't approve of my opinions . . ."

"Just keep them to yourself, okay? What do you think Mac would say if he knew you were encouraging Beatrice to fight Alice?"

Rachel spun around, her eyes flashing with anger. "Mac has nothing to do with this." The very last thing she wanted was for her husband to get involved. Although Rachel knew that Mac loved her, she knew, too, that he was particularly sympathetic to Alice. In fact, it was Mac who had encouraged her to make her peace with Alice at long last. As much as Rachel believed that Sally belonged with Beatrice, she was also afraid to risk her husband's disapproval if he didn't agree.

Ada leveled her daughter with a forboding look. "I'm warning you, Rachel, if Mac finds out that you've been butting into Alice's life again, it's going to cause trouble in your marriage. And if Iris finds out and tells him . . . well, you know what will happen."

Deep down, Rachel knew that her mother meant well,

46

and thus took her warning seriously. On the one hand, Rachel didn't want to do anything to cause the slightest tension in her marriage, especially now that she was pregnant. Mac Cory was all that she could ever hope for in a man and more: a confidant, friend and lover, he was the mainstay of her life. And in just a few short months, they would have their first child. Rachel didn't want to rock the boat, or give Iris an excuse to do it for her. Mac's daughter was obviously getting fairly desperate, but Rachel was determined not to let Iris drive her and Mac apart. In fact, the baby she was carrying could even make their relationship more solid, and perhaps, Rachel reasoned, that was why Iris would do anything, tell any lie to cause a rift between her and Mac.

On the other hand, there was also Beatrice Gordon to consider. Sally deserved to know the truth, and Beatrice deserved to have her granddaughter. Alice Frame would just have to accept that, Rachel told herself. She could always adopt another child; Sally only had one grandmother.

That evening, Rachel had a long talk with her housekeeper. "I think you should get in touch with your son," Rachel advised.

"But what will I tell him?" Beatrice asked, somewhat helplessly.

"Tell him to come to Bay City. You're going to need all the family you've got around you for the next few months."

Beatrice considered the suggestion carefully. Rachel was right. Besides, Raymond was a lawyer and would be the best one to advise her on how to proceed. Moreover, Beatrice was certain that once her son knew about Sally, he would be on the next plane to Bay City without hesitation. The only stumbling block might be his wife, Olive, whose main mission in life seemed to be to keep Raymond away from his mother. For that, Beatrice would never forgive her

47

daughter-in-law. Alone in her room, she waited for the late night telephone rates to go into effect and then dialed her son's number.

"Raymond? I—I hope I'm not calling you too late?" Beatrice began haltingly.

"It's only eight o'clock here, Mom," he replied with a laugh. "There's nothing wrong is there?" he asked, his husky voice sounding concerned.

"Son, I need your help," Beatrice blurted out. "I need you to come to Bay City right away!"

Chapter Four
Loose Ends

Dark, snow-filled clouds hung over Bay City as Raymond Gordon's taxi sped to the Avery Hotel, which was in the most fashionable part of town. His mother's call had troubled him. In recent years, she had become increasingly more preoccupied with his sister, Jennifer, and her death. A brooding sense of guilt seemed to have overtaken her. It was as if she were desperate to bring back the past, as if she would have done anything to have just one more chance to be a mother to Jenny again. Whenever they spoke over the phone, Jenny would invariably figure into the conversation somehow. That was why this latest call was so disturbing. Beatrice could not have Jenny, but she now appeared determined to have a substitute. But a granddaughter suddenly materializing from out of the blue? That was plain ridiculous.

When Ray arrived at the hotel, two messages greeted him. The first was from his wife, Olive, instructing him to call home immediately. The other was from his mother, instructing him to call her immediately. Raymond took a quarter out of his pocket and laughed lightly. *This is a situation best approached with some humor,* he told himself as he tossed the coin: heads, he'd call Olive first; tails, his mother. Raymond looked at the coin in his palm and smiled.

"You lose, Olive," he muttered with no little satisfaction. As expected, his wife had not made his departure an easy one. The mere fact that his coming to Bay City involved Beatrice annoyed Olive no end.

"She'll never stop interfering in our lives," Olive warned in that ugly, droning tone she used whenever the subject of her mother-in-law came up. It was true that when Beatrice had lived in California, she'd tended to be overprotective where her son and grandsons were concerned. In fact, she was a real pain most of the time. But Beatrice was Raymond's mother, and he knew she had not had it very easy in recent years. As a result, he was more disposed to take her eccentricities with patience and good-naturedness than Olive was. Olive didn't see things quite that way but, Raymond thought as he dialed his mother's number, that was Olive's problem.

"I'm here, Mom," Raymond said when she answered, happy to hear the note of relief in his mother's voice.

"Thank goodness. Now, Ray, I want you to come right over to the Corys' house; I'm going to cook you a good, nourishing dinner," Bea instructed.

Raymond had to smile to himself. Wasn't that just like a mother? "Nothing doing," he replied. "Tonight I'm taking you out on the town. You get out your best dress and be ready at six-thirty, okay?"

"But, Raymond, we have so much to talk about!"

"What's the matter, we can't talk over dinner?" he teased.

"Sweetheart, I told you what it's about. It's serious. We have to come to a decision!"

Raymond let out a long, troubled sigh. He'd been afraid of this—afraid that his mother would be so obsessed by the thought of having a granddaughter that she wouldn't be able to see past it. He had hoped to put her in a more relaxed frame of mind before talking about it. Maybe a fancy dinner and a good bottle of wine. But as usual, Beatrice was having none of it.

"I'm taking you out, Mom, I don't want any arguing," Raymond said in a firm, authoritative voice that he hoped would convince her.

"Well . . . if you insist," Beatrice replied haltingly. "I suppose a night out would be a pleasant change, especially since I'll be with my handsome son!"

Raymond's warm brown eyes sparkled. Even at his age, he was a sucker for his mother's compliments. He remembered back to the time in high school when he was the quarterback for the Hamilton High football team. Beatrice didn't understand a thing about the game, but she sat in the bleachers religiously every Saturday afternoon, beaming, poking the man or woman next to her. "See that good-looking young man with number nine on his back? That's my boy!" she'd brag.

"Don't forget to wear your dancing shoes," Raymond reminded his mother just before he hung up. He remembered how she used to love to dance as a young woman.

"Oh, Raymond, you are crazy," Beatrice giggled delightedly. She hung up the phone and smiled. Everything was going to be fine now that her son was in town. The only big problem as she saw it was having to deal with Alice Frame. That was one confrontation Beatrice was not looking forward to.

The next morning, Alice Frame felt like a new woman. For the first time in days, the sun was shining, making the snow that had piled up in the yard shimmer like mounds of spun glass. She felt good about the way her talk with Beatrice had gone and was sure the woman would do nothing to jeopardize the adoption proceedings. In a few short weeks, Sally Spenser could officially change her last name to

Frame. Alice smiled to herself as she sipped her mug of piping hot coffee. *Steven would have been very pleased,* she told herself, *if only he had lived to see this day.*

Although Steven Frame has been missing for months, since his plane went down in the South American jungles, somehow in her heart Alice had never given up hope that one day he would come back to her. Her head told her that it was a foolish hope, but when you loved someone as deeply and totally as she had loved Steven, you had to listen to your heart. But, she had made up her mind not to brood about it. A whole new, exciting life stretched out in front of her, and Alice was determined to live it to the fullest. Adopting Sally was going to be the first step.

Alice went over to the hall closet and took a small, slim jewelry box from the top shelf. Luckily Sally was not tall enough to reach the top shelf yet, Alice realized with some measure of amusement. Otherwise, she would have most certainly discovered her birthday present by now. Alice opened the box and traced her fingers lovingly over the delicate gold ID bracelet. In flowing script, it read: "Sally Frame."

"Alice, have you had your breakfast yet?" Sally's voice called from the kitchen. Quickly, Alice returned the gift to it's hiding place, just as Sally entered. She was wearing the long red and blue plaid nightshirt Alice's Aunt Liz had bought for her when they went on their monthly shopping spree.

"Just coffee. I was waiting for you, sleepyhead," she replied, tousling Sally's long, straight blond hair.

"It's Saturday, remember? I can sleep late today."

"Sure, but I thought you were going to make breakfast for your old Mom."

"C'mon, you're not old, Alice. You look great. Almost like a teenager, that's what Billy Fergeson said."

Alice tried to stifle a smile. It was common knowledge in middle school circles that young Billy had a real crush on

Sally and would've said just about anything to get her attention, including wild flattery. "Tell Billy Fergeson that he's a gentleman and a scholar—and a terrific liar."

"He's a jerk, if you ask me. But he does carry my books, so I guess he's good for something."

Alice shook her head in mock horror. "You're terrible!"

Sally shrugged. "I know," she said with a girlish giggle. "Now, how does scrambled eggs and toast sound?"

"If you're cooking, I'm eating," Alice proclaimed and followed her soon-to-be daughter into the kitchen. Yes, she thought, things were definitely looking up.

Under the best of conditions, it was no treat to be sitting in the waiting room at Bay City General Hospital. But considering Pat's reason for being there, it was downright awful. As she watched the patients, many of them seriously ill, hobbling or being wheeled down the corridor, she knew she should be thankful she was in good health, physically at any rate. As far as her mental state at this moment was concerned, she couldn't quite vouch for that.

"You can go in now, Mrs. Randolph. Dr. Gilchrist is waiting," the nurse said, wearing a predictable, plastic smile that was supposed to make people feel comforted and secure, but only made Pat feel more depressed than she was to begin with.

"Pat, I'm so glad you came," Dave said, holding out a chair for her.

"I hate to be such a bother, Dave," she began apologetically.

Dave put his hand over hers. "I don't ever want to hear you say that. I told you in New York that I'm here for you any time, day or night, and I meant it. I care about you, Pat, please believe that."

"I do and I'm grateful," Pat said, smiling back. "You've been my anchor through all of this. I couldn't have made it without knowing you were a phone call away." Truly, just knowing that Dave knew her secret made Pat's burden seem lighter. Being caught in between John and Marianne was bad enough, but if she hadn't had anyone to share her dilemma with, it would have been impossible. It would have been like those terrible months, years ago, when John had taken up with Bernice. Back then, however, Pat had turned to vodka to ease her pain.

"Have you spoken to Marianne recently about her telling John?" Dave asked after pausing to give Pat a few moments to compose herself.

"I've tried, Dave. But every time I try to have a word with her, she races out of the house on some pretext or other," Pat replied wearily.

"You can't go on like this," Dave warned, his voice concerned. "You've got to make her listen."

"I'm really worried about John, too," Pat said at last.

"Do you think he suspects the truth?"

"He knows something isn't right. For heaven's sake, I'm not right!"

Dave looked at her, puzzled. "What do you mean, Pat?"

It was difficult for her to talk about such personal things, but Pat needed to tell someone and it might as well be Dave Gilchrist, who was at least sympathetic.

"I haven't been much of a wife in these past few weeks," she admitted, her voice barely a whisper. For a long moment, she could not bring herself to look at Dave. She felt so embarrassed. *What must he think of me?* she asked herself as her eyes stared at the gloomy gray hospital carpet.

"I can see you're very tense. I'm sure John must sense it too," Dave replied diplomatically.

"He keeps doing these nice things, planning evenings out or making time for me in his busy schedule, but . . ." Her voice trailed off.

"Maybe you just need some time by yourself," Dave offered. "To sort out your feelings. Why not go away for a few days? Visit a friend. It might put things in a whole new perspective for you."

"Do you really think so?" Pat asked, perking up a bit.

"I think it might. Although I must confess, I'll miss having you to talk to while you're gone."

Pat felt her cheeks getting hot. That night at her hotel in New York, she had felt the same way when Dave looked at her with those dark, bottomless eyes of his. It was almost as if he could see right through her, as if he could search out every secret place inside of her. Then, as now, her heart was racing and consciously, at least, she did not quite know why.

"Maybe I'll give Lisa Palmer a call," Pat decided. "She was my best friend in high school. I just got a card from her last week. She's just gotten a big job with the national gallery in Washington. I'd love to spend some time with her."

"There you are. That's perfect," Dave replied. "I'll bet you'll feel like a new woman when you get back!"

I only hope so, Pat thought as she left Dave's office. Now, how was she ever going to explain another trip out of town to John, that was the question. The answer was fairly obvious: she couldn't. John would never understand.

"Pat, you just came back from New York!" John cried incredulously when his wife informed him of her plans to go to Washington, D.C.

"It's only for a few days, John. Besides, I haven't seen Lisa in over ten years. It's a wonderful opportunity."

"What about me? What about our life together? Doesn't that matter to you?"

"Of course it does," she insisted. "But as I said, I won't be long."

"You know we were invited to Sally's birthday party tomorrow night. What'll Alice think if you're not there?"

"I explained everything to Alice when I spoke with her earlier, and I assure you, she understands. Why don't you go to the party anyway?"

"I'm not going to go by myself," John protested. "How would that look?"

Pat knew from the plaintive tone in his voice that John was just trying to get her to change her mind, but Pat refused to be swayed. This time she had to think of her own well-being first. Otherwise, she had better forget about everything, including her marriage. Dave was right. A few days away from Bay City and all her problems was bound to give Pat a fresh perspective on everything. When she got back, she would deal with things once and for all. But right now, her mind was too jumbled up to even clearly define her options. She was going to Washington and that was final.

"I'm sorry, John, but I really want to go."

"And that's it?" he asked, his voice filled with amazement.

"Yes, I'm afraid it is."

It was past three thirty, and Alice knew Aunt Liz wasn't going to be able to keep Sally out indefinitely. Certainly not on her birthday, she mused as she rushed around the living room, putting some finishing touches on the last of the party decorations. Alice was determined to make this the best birthday that Sally had ever had. Since it was a surprise party, it was even more important that everything be exactly right. Aunt Liz had promised to keep Sally busy with a birthday lunch and then shopping until at least six o'clock, but the guests were supposed to arrive at five-thirty. That sure didn't give Alice much time. She hadn't picked up the cake yet, or the trays of cold cuts from the caterer. And from the looks of the gray, January sky, another snowfall was imminent.

Grabbing her car keys, Alice made a mad dash to the door, flung it open and was surprised to come face to face with a tall, handsome man, whose finger was poised to ring the doorbell. They both laughed awkwardly.

"Guess I beat you to it," Alice said, somewhat out of breath.

"You must be Alice Frame," Ray Gordon replied in his easy, laid-back California drawl.

"Yes, I am," she answered, "but I'm afraid you have the advantage, Mr.—"

"I'm sorry. Gordon, Ray Gordon. I'm Beatrice's son from California." He held out his bare hand.

"Oh," Alice said, slightly unnerved. She shook his hand. It was smooth and strong, but cold from the icy air. "I was just on my way out," she explained.

"I know. I . . . should have called first," Ray stammered, "but to tell you the truth . . . I wasn't sure you'd see me if I did."

Alice could feel a lump of fear forming in her throat. For a brief moment, she had almost let herself be convinced that everything was going to work out, that the adoption was going to go through without a hitch and she and Sally were going to be a family. The look in Ray Gordon's resolute brown eyes told her differently.

"Please come in, Mr. Gordon," Alice said, trying to control the shaking in her voice.

"I suppose you can guess why I've come," he offered in a thoroughly unchallenging tone.

"About Sally, naturally." They walked into the living room, and Alice's heart immediately sank as her eyes surveyed the party decor. *What a time for something like this to happen,* she reflected. *Some birthday party this is going to be.*

"Looks like somebody's having a birthday," Ray said, trying to sound cheerful.

"It's for Sally, today's her birthday. It's a surprise party."

The tone of defeat in Alice's voice cut Ray to the quick. In all honesty, he had come to have a very matter-of-fact, very business-like discussion with Mrs. Frame. But when he saw the way her beautiful heart-shaped face had clouded with pain, he knew this was not going to be an easy conversation. He also knew that he was going to have a hard time getting this woman out of his mind when he left.

After Ray had explained his mother's position, Alice fell silent. In the back of her mind she was aware that Beatrice had every right to adopt her daughter's child, but somehow she'd never thought it would come to that. Certainly Beatrice hadn't given her that impression after they'd spoken. In fact, Alice had promised to tell Sally the truth and had also assured Beatrice that she hoped and expected that she would want to be a grandmother to Sally in every way. That seemed to have been enough for Beatrice, but obviously Alice had been mistaken.

"Why would a woman of her age even want the responsibility of raising a child?" Alice asked when she was finally able to pull her thoughts together.

"Sally is her natural granddaughter, Mrs. Frame. I'm afraid she has every right to want custody of her," Ray replied.

"That's no answer," Alice insisted. "Sally loves me and I love her. I already told Beatrice that she could spend as much time with Sally as she wanted. Why isn't that good enough?"

"Sally's mother, my sister Jennifer, left home when she was quite young, Mrs. Frame. It broke my mother's heart. I suppose she sees Sally as a substitute for Jennifer."

"Sally has her own identity, Mr. Gordon. Why would you or Beatrice want to take that away from her?"

"I don't, I assure you. And I think it's a little premature to be even discussing all this. Why don't we just keep it simple for now?"

"Simple how, Mr. Gordon?"

"Well, you could call me Ray or Raymond for starters," he began with a smile. "Then you could introduce me to Sally. I never had a niece before. What do you say?"

"I say . . . how would you like to eat some birthday cake tonight? Provided I can still make it to the bakery and pick it up, that is."

"Well then, let's get going. We've got a party to go to!"

Despite her reservations, and despite the fact that Ray had to go to the baker's house and practically beg him to re-open the store and give them Sally's cake, things went well. Alice breathed a sigh of relief when Aunt Liz escorted Sally into the Frame living room, turned on the lights and everyone yelled out: "Surprise!" Sally was absolutely thrilled. In her words, she was, "completely wiped out." All Alice knew was that her little girl had on a prize-winning smile that stretched from ear to ear, and that was what Alice cared about.

Ray Gordon fit right in, too. He helped dish out the ice cream, and re-inflate balloons. He was an old hand at this kind of thing, Alice noted with genuine admiration, just as Steven would have been. However, it was no day for dark and dreary thoughts, so Alice pushed them right out of her head and joined in the fun. And to her utter astonishment, she actually found she was having a good time. So was Ray, who cut the three-layer chocolate marshmallow cake while Alice tried to hold the plates close enough that he wouldn't spill anything on the table. More than once they caught each other's gaze, and if Alice wasn't about to admit what she felt, Ray Gordon had no such reservation. He was captivated. Absolutely captivated.

Beatrice, however, was not one bit pleased at her son's behavior. Oh, she liked Alice, but Raymond was still a married man and with this business about Sally looming over them, his developing any kind of friendship with her would only complicate matters. Rachel Cory was in complete agreement with her housekeeper.

"I really think you should speak to Ray," she whispered to Beatrice. "You know Alice is very vulnerable right now, what with Steve gone and all."

"I know. Raymond's always been foolish where women were concerned," Beatrice sighed. "Olive is proof positive of that!"

From another corner of the room, Iris Delaney watched Rachel with rapt interest, taking the opportunity to draw Liz Matthews over.

"I don't know why Rachel always has to stir up trouble," Iris said, shaking her perfectly coifed head in mock dismay.

"Why don't you ask Mac to speak to her?" Liz inquired. "He would have a fit if he knew Rachel was trying to make Alice's life unbearable."

Iris patted Liz on the arm reassuringly. "I'll do what I can, dear. You know how much I want to help poor Alice."

Just before it was time to open the gifts, John Randolph arrived with Barbara Weaver. Liz's eyes almost popped out of their sockets. She pulled Alice aside immediately.

"What is he doing here with that *woman?*"

Alice shrugged. "Pat's out of town, and I guess John just didn't want to come alone."

"Alice, how could you let him do this to your own sister?" Liz demanded to know.

"Aunt Liz, I haven't done anything, and neither has John or Barbara."

"This is Bernice Kline all over again," Liz moaned. "I'm sure of it."

"Would you please calm down, Aunt Liz. They'll hear you," Alice insisted.

But it didn't look like Liz was about to be silenced so easily. "If you won't ask that woman to leave, then I will," she said as she started toward John and Barbara. Alice grabbed her aunt roughly by the arm.

"Don't you dare! This is my house, Aunt Liz, and this is Sally's party. I will not have you causing a scene, is that clear?"

Liz leveled her niece with a disapproving glare and would have objected, but Alice stopped her.

"If you do anything to disrupt Sally's party, I'll never forgive you!"

Liz inhaled deeply. "Why do you all always accuse me of disrupting things when all I ever want to do is make sure everyone is happy?" she mumbled as she turned away.

She looked across the room and saw Marianne helping herself at the buffet table. Making a bee-line over to her great-niece, Liz seemed determined that someone in the family was going to be made to see reason before the night was over. But Marianne was no more cooperative than anyone else.

"Dad and Barbara are good friends. What's wrong with that?" Marianne snapped when Liz started to imply otherwise.

"Why are you defending that woman?" Liz asked in astonishment. "Don't you care that your own mother is being made to look like a fool?"

"You're way off base, Aunt Liz," Marianne warned.

Once again, Liz wasn't going to be put off that easily. "You know Pat's started seeing Dr. Gilchrist. Aren't you even concerned about why?"

"It was . . . just a routine checkup," Marianne covered. She didn't want anyone to know the real reason her mother had become acquainted with Dr. Gilchrist.

"How do you know that?"

Marianne stammered, wanting to change the subject. "Because . . . what else could it be?"

Liz arched her brow and looked directly at John, who

was helping Barbara to a piece of cake. "I can think of one very good reason."

Later, when it was time to open the gifts, everyone crowded around Sally. Ray put himself in charge of wrapping-paper disposal, while Alice was set to weave the ribbons together into a giant birthday corsage that Sally could keep as a momento. Sally herself was bursting with excitement. Her big blue eyes widened with wonder at each successive gift. But when she came to Alice's present, her whole face lit up.

"Oh, Alice! I love it," Sally cried, staring at the bracelet. "It's the best birthday present I ever had!" She ran over and hugged Alice. Beatrice fixed her son with an angry look. She had a mind to tell Sally right then and there that she was a Gordon, not a Frame. And she never would be a Frame if Beatrice had anything to say about it. But it was not the time. She wouldn't have spoiled Sally's birthday for anything.

"Look, Mrs. Gordon," Sally chirped, showing her the bracelet. "Isn't it the most beautiful thing you've ever seen?"

Beatrice smiled wanly. "It's very lovely, Sally."

Alice nodded at Beatrice in silent gratitude. At least they both seemed to have the child's welfare at heart. They could tell Sally about her real family tomorrow.

"I'd just like to say thank you to everybody for coming," the birthday girl announced. "I especially want to say a big thank you to my new mom." Sally turned to face Alice. "I really love you a lot!" They gave each other a big hug as Beatrice watched, biting her lip. Ray was quick to notice.

"Take it easy, Mom," he whispered. "There's nothing to be jealous about."

"I just want my granddaughter. Is there anything wrong with that?"

"Not a thing. Just keep it all in perspective, okay?"

Beatrice patted her son's hand. "I will, don't you worry. I'm not going to spoil Sally's party."

"That thought never crossed my mind," Ray replied, knowing full well all his mother needed was a little provocation. But after meeting Alice and Sally, he was going to do his damnedest to see that Beatrice made things as painless for them as possible. As for his young niece, Ray Gordon was absolutely won over. After ten minutes of re-inflating half-dead balloons together, they were fast friends.

"You haven't even opened my present yet," Rachel suddenly said in mock disappointment.

"Yes, I did," Sally replied, reaching for the riding costume that had come in a fancy box from one of the specialty stores in town. The card read: "To Sally, Happy Birthday! Love, Rachel and Mac." Sally held the outfit up in front of herself.

"That's going to look might spiffy on you, young lady," Mac observed.

"Now all I need is a horse!" Sally said, laughing.

"Well, I was wondering when you were going to get around to that," Rachel replied. "It just so happens that there's an adorable new calico pony at the Cory Stables, and I do believe he's almost exactly the right size for you. You can come over and ride him any time."

"Are you serious?" Sally cried, full of excitement.

"Of course. He doesn't have a name yet, though. Maybe you could do the honor," Rachel continued.

Sally stood up and threw her arms around Mrs. Cory. "Oh, Rachel, thank you so much. Wait'll the kids at school hear about this! It's the best birthday present I ever had!"

The party continued, and Alice finally found an opportunity to draw Rachel aside. "It was lovely of you, but I wish you had mentioned the pony to me first," Alice said.

"It was quite extravagant of you." She hoped Rachel wouldn't take offense, but she had to say something. She didn't want Sally to grow up expecting such lavish gifts for every birthday.

"I thought you'd want Sally to have access to the stables," Rachel replied, surprised by the other woman's comment.

"That's not the point. It's just that you were very generous—too generous—and I think you should have consulted me."

"If you don't want Sally to have the outfit and the use of the stables, of course I'll understand. I never meant to offend you, Alice," Rachel apologized, feeling suddenly terrible.

"Forget it, okay? It's a lovely gift and obviously Sally's very excited about it. Just ask next time."

Rachel bit her lip as Alice walked over to join Sally and Ray, who was helping her put all her gifts away. No matter how hard she tried, the Matthews family was never going to think she was good enough, Rachel thought with frustration. Even an innocent gift for a child became an object of criticism. Fortunately, Mac understood.

"You were just trying a little too hard, honey, that's all. Next time, you'll know better."

"Oh, Mac, I'm sorry. I only wanted to do something special for Sally!"

"You should have asked Alice first, but I'm sure she understands." He hugged her lightly to him. "Now this is supposed to be a party. Let's not discuss it any further."

Rachel watched as Mac walked away. She loved him so much, and now she'd disappointed him. She'd done something, no matter how well intended, that had made him uncomfortable. *Oh, when will I ever learn?* she wondered.

"I think the pony was a lovely idea, Mrs. Cory," Beatrice said as she walked over to Rachel. "Don't mind the others. They're just jealous!"

Rachel gave her housekeeper a warm hug. "Thanks, I needed that," she said sincerely.

What she didn't need was Iris's continued efforts to destroy her marriage to Mac, she thought as she noticed Iris take her father's arm and whisper something to him. Anytime Rachel turned her back, Iris was right there trying to put a knife in. Well, Rachel told herself, it was going to stop. She would tell Mac what she knew about Iris and her threats that if Clarice ever told Robert he was Cory's father, Iris would make her wish she hadn't. Then Mac would banish his daughter from the Cory house and his life forever. Rachel smiled. Let Iris think she had the upper hand for now. Rachel knew better.

Across the room, Iris helped Mac to a second piece of birthday cake.

"I really shouldn't," Mac protested.

"Oh, Daddy, you're much too handsome to worry about putting on an extra pound or two," Iris said as she fed him a forkful. Mac gave his daughter a hug.

"You know I love it when you fuss over me. I just wish we could be like this all the time, instead of—"

"Instead of what?" Iris challenged, her face a mask of indignation.

"I wish you could try to get along with Rachel, Iris. She's my wife and I love her, no matter what you might think."

Iris arched her eyebrow. What she thought was how well Rachel had manipulated Mac into believing he cared for her. The woman had a well-known history for being a liar and a tramp, and Iris was smart enough to realize that those things never changed. Rachel had married Mac for two things: money and social position. And by the time Iris was finished with her, she wasn't going to have either.

"Daddy, I have tried to be friendly with Rachel, but she makes it impossible," Iris began sweetly. "Well, look what she's done tonight; it's a perfect example. She doesn't care who she hurts. Look at how much she's upset Alice."

Mac frowned. He knew in his heart that Rachel hadn't meant any harm, that she was trying to make up for all her past sins, but she did have a knack for doing and saying the wrong things. He indulgently blamed it on her youth and lack of experience. After all, he was old enough to be her father and, like a parent, forgave a lot where his beautiful wife was concerned.

"I hope you realize that I'm not trying to speak up against Rachel," Iris said, looking at her father with wide, innocent eyes. "I just wish she wouldn't embarrass you so. And in public, too." Iris watched her father stiffen and inwardly congratulated herself on a job well done. If there was one thing Mac Cory valued, it was the high opinion of his friends. To have Rachel at his side as a constant embarrassment was bound to take it's toll sooner or later. And tonight, Iris told herself, Rachel had helped herself to a huge portion of chagrin. Now all Iris had to do was help it along just a bit and she knew exactly how to accomplish that.

Her name was Tracey DeWitt. . . .

Chapter Five
Tug-of-War

Meeting his niece, Sally, for the first time had made quite an impact on Ray Gordon. In fact, the whole atmosphere in the Frame house had surprised him. Sally and Alice were definitely a loving family unit, and in his heart he knew it would be wrong to do anything to change or jeopardize that. But there were also Beatrice's feelings to consider. His mother was completely set and determined to raise Sally herself, and though he didn't doubt for a moment that his mother's intentions were the best, he had to question her suitability to be a mother to Sally. First off, her age was against her. As Alice had astutely pointed out, she was hardly young anymore. But there was more than that to consider. There was the whole reason Jennifer had left home in the first place.

Ada McGowan was the perfect sounding board for Ray's misgivings. Not only was Ada his mother's good friend, but she was also a friend of Alice's. And from all reports, he knew her to be a fair woman. The morning after Sally's party, Ray and Ada sat down to coffee in her kitchen. As he'd expected, Ada was sympathetic. But he wasn't aware that she, too, had misgivings about what his mother planned to do.

"I don't think my mother would make an appropriate guardian for a girl Sally's age," Ray began.

Ada laughed good-humoredly. "Watch it, Ray, you're looking at an old lady who has a little girl herself." Ada was referring to her young daughter, Nancy, who had been the unplanned but happy result of her marriage to Gil McGowan. But though Ada loved her child to distraction, she would have been the first to admit that at her stage in life, it was no easy task to get back into the routine of baking brownies for nursery school and showing up at PTA meetings with mothers twenty years her junior. Ray, however, had not even thought about that. Instead, he had concentrated on something else, something that made Beatrice completely unsuited to the task.

"My mother is the reason Jenny left home," Ray blurted out.

"What do you mean?" Ada asked, obviously surprised. "How?"

"She was always at her," Ray began. "I guess you could say she stifled the poor kid with affection, twenty-four hours a day. She had no time to herself, no friends. She had to do nearly everything with Mom or not do it at all."

Ray was in college at the time, but he recalled when he would come home on weekends or for semester breaks how Jenny was always in a state of depression. Beatrice wouldn't let her go on trips with her school friends, she couldn't have dates, she couldn't even go out shopping by herself. As a result, Jenny began to sneak around.

"My sister got in with a bad crowd, and that was the beginning of the end, I'm afraid."

Ada nodded sympathetically. "That's what happens when you're overprotective with a kid. I'm sorry, Ray, I had no idea."

Neither did anyone else, Ray thought sadly. If any judge knew Beatrice's history with her own daughter, there was no way on this earth she would be awarded custody of Sally. And if Ray had sized up the situation with Alice correctly, he was quite sure that she would leave no stone unturned if it came down to a fight for the little girl. And he was very much afraid for his mother if she did.

Later that day, Ray went to see Scott Bradley.

"Your mother hasn't made an official petition to challenge Sally's adoption," Scott informed him.

"But she has indicated to you that she intends to do that," Ray added rather bluntly.

"I think that is her intention, but I counseled her to speak to Alice first and try and resolve things without a legal battle. As you know, this kind of thing can get very messy."

Since he was a lawyer himself, Ray knew exactly what Scott meant. Custody fights were downright ugly and in the end, the child was always the loser. On the other hand, Sally was a Gordon, and Ray believed that she should be raised by her own family, if that was possible. Beatrice, however, was not the right choice for a mother.

"I've got to be honest with you, Scott," Ray said at last. "I don't think my mother should have custody of Sally, but I do think the child should be with our family."

"What are you suggesting?" Scott asked, baffled.

"I've got to speak to my wife first, of course, but I'm thinking of adopting Sally myself. After all, she is my niece and we do have a lovely home in California where I'm sure Sally would be very happy."

"Again, Ray, I think that whatever you decide, it's best to try to avoid a legal tug-of-war, if possible."

"Oh, I have every intention of speaking to Alice Frame," Ray assured his colleague. "In fact, I'm going to ask her to dinner tonight and see if we can resolve this quickly and painlessly." Of course, part of Ray knew that any attempt to convince Alice to give up Sally would be completely fruitless. The other, unconscious, part just wanted an excuse to be with the lovely Mrs. Frame again.

But Ray was out of luck. When he called the Frame house, there was no answer. After that, he dialed his wife, Olive, who was anything but receptive to her husband's idea of bringing her a new child to care for.

"Don't I have my hands full enough now with the boys?" Olive complained. "As it is I never have time to have my hair done or go to the club with my friends. There is no way I'm going to take care of your sister's brat, too. You can just forget it!" Olive cried, slamming down the phone.

Ray felt his face heating with anger. His relationship with Olive was growing more and more strained. It was true that he spent a good deal of time away from home, either taking cases out of town or just preferring to work late at the office. But when he was there, Ray was finding life in his own home increasingly intolerable. The only thing Olive cared about was her own comfort. She was constantly complaining that he didn't earn enough money, that their house wasn't big enough, that her clothes weren't chic enough. If the truth were known, she would probably be a worse mother to Sally than Beatrice could ever be. But at least Ray would be there to make sure his niece was being treated well. For even with Olive's incessant litany of woes, he knew she would do as he asked so long as he provided her with enough money. But even as the thought crossed his mind, he knew in his heart that his niece was far better off with Alice Frame. Now, if he had a wife like Alice, everything would be perfect. Yes, Ray thought to himself for more reasons than one, if only . . .

When Ray told his mother of his decision, she was devastated.

"How could you do this to me?" she asked, shocked that

her own son would try to keep her away from her grand-daughter.

"I just think it would be better for Sally if she had a more conventional home life," Ray tried to explain.

"There's nothing conventional about that wife of yours," Beatrice snapped. "She's already turned your sons against me. Do you really think I'll stand by and let her do the same thing with Sally?"

"You could move back to California," Ray offered. "That way, we'd be like a real family again. You could see Sally anytime you liked."

Beatrice sat up straight on the antique sofa in the Corys' living room. She leveled her son with a cold, angry glare. "If you don't mind, Raymond, I have my chores to do before Mrs. Cory gets home."

Aware that he had just been dismissed, Ray stood up with an uneasy heart. "I'm not trying to hurt you, Mom, you've got to believe that. I'm trying to do what's best for everyone. After all, Sally's the most important consideration here."

"You think I don't have her best interests at heart?"

"Yes, I'm sure you do. But be realistic. Where would the two of you live? You certainly don't earn enough working here to be able to pay rent somewhere and support Sally."

Ray's words had stung Beatrice to the quick. Her own son was practically telling her that she was unfit to raise Sally. He had also successfully managed to call back all her own initial reservations. It was true enough that she was only a housekeeper, and had no real place of her own except the small bedroom and sitting room that came with her position. Certainly she would have to find a place for herself and Sally. And then there was the question of the child's schooling and clothing.

Beatrice put her hand to her forehead. The whole situation was just a little overwhelming. Maybe Raymond had been right all along. Maybe she wasn't the right person to have custody of her granddaughter. But once again, it was Rachel who convinced her otherwise.

"That's just fear talking," she assured Beatrice. "The main thing is that you have your granddaughter. The rest will work itself out."

"But how will I support her?" Beatrice asked, genuinely concerned.

"Mac and I will give you all the help you need, you know that."

"But I couldn't accept charity. It wouldn't be right."

Rachel touched her arm to reassure her. "Why don't we just cross that bridge when we come to it? The important thing now is to get your petition started," she reminded her gently. "Call Scott, before it's too late, Beatrice."

Beatrice buried her head in her hands. "I'm so confused. I don't know what to do!"

"If Alice's adoption goes through while you're sitting here making up your mind, you'll never forgive yourself. You'll lose Sally forever. Is that a risk you're willing to take?"

The very idea was like a knife being plunged into Beatrice's heart. The memory of her dear, beautiful Jenny was still so strong in her mind. When she'd discovered the girl had run away from home, it had nearly destroyed Beatrice. Jenny was her bright, shining star in the darkness. She had been her only reason to live and when Jenny was gone so, too, had the light in Beatrice's life been extinguished. Sally was her chance to start all over again. From the moment she found out that the girl was her granddaughter, Beatrice had felt a new enthusiasm for life. She couldn't give that up. She couldn't deny it, either. Not now. Rachel was right. Beatrice could wait no longer, or she would indeed regret it for the rest of her life.

Purposefully, she dialed Scott Bradley's number.

"I want to begin the proceedings for custody of Sally immediately," she informed the attorney.

"Have you talked this over with Alice as I asked you to?" Scott questioned.

"We spoke once. I don't think it would serve any purpose to talk again. You see, neither one of us is about to give in. I want my granddaughter and that's all there is to it!"

Beatrice felt a lot better after the phone call. Scott had assured her that he would draw up the necessary papers and present them to John Randolph immediately. Whether the case went to court or not was entirely dependent upon Alice and Beatrice. And as Beatrice said, neither of them was about to cave in; a long and nasty fight seemed inevitable. But Beatrice was set in her resolve. As long as there was a chance she could have Sally, nothing else mattered. The only problem now, it appeared, was to convince her son to drop the foolish notion that *he* should adopt the girl.

When his mother invited him over for dinner that evening, Ray appeared hopeful. Rachel had graciously offered the west wing dining room for their privacy, and she'd instructed the cook to prepare them a wonderful meal. Although Beatrice was a little uncomfortable in such oppulent surroundings, she forced herself to put on a good face for her son.

"I'm glad you want to talk this out," Ray said, breaking the silence. "I never meant to alienate you, Mom."

Beatrice held her ground. "That's exactly what you did, Raymond. In fact, you did a lot more. You insinuated that I wouldn't be a fit guardian for Sally."

Ray took his mother's hands gently in his and kissed them. "I love you more than anything. You know that," he told her softly. "The last thing I want is for you to be unhappy."

"If I don't have Sally, I will be, Raymond."

"Mom, think of Sally, will you?"

"That's why I'm doing this," Beatrice insisted, her eyes beginning to fill with tears. "She's my Jenny's baby. I can't just let her go."

"But don't you remember how it was with Jenny, Mom?" Ray asked gently, not wanting to hurt her feelings any more than he already had.

"It was wonderful. We were inseparable!"

"That was the problem, Mom. You didn't let her have a life of her own. You know that's why she fell in with the wrong bunch."

Beatrice swallowed hard. What Ray was saying was true. She had been a bit overbearing with her daughter. Perhaps if she hadn't been quite so strict, the whole tragedy could have been averted. But that was over and done with, and no matter how many times Beatrice went over in her mind what she had done wrong, it wasn't going to bring her little Jenny back. The girl had left her and died alone. It was a cross Beatrice had learned to bear, but with Sally at least there was now the hope of redemption—a chance to start over.

"All I want is another chance," Beatrice explained. "I know I made mistakes with Jenny, but that's not going to happen this time."

"Mom, you're the same person. You'll probably be even more protective with Sally because of what happened to Jenny," Ray reasoned.

But Beatrice wasn't listening. "You're wrong, Raymond. With Sally I'll have a second chance. I'll be able to make it up to Jenny in some small way by raising her daughter to be a fine young woman. Please Raymond," she begged, the tears streaming down her cheeks, "please don't take that away from me. It's all I have left, all I can give to my poor baby girl!"

Ray hugged his mother tightly to him. The love she felt

for Sally was obvious. He also understood her reasons for wanting to adopt her. And although he still had very strong, nagging reservations, he gave in.

"All right. I'll withdraw my custody action. If it means this much to you, maybe I was wrong." Beatrice was ecstatic. She kissed her son in gratitude. At last, she was going to have her chance, she thought. Jenny was going to come back to her, if only in spirit.

"Thank you, Raymond," she cried. "You've made me the happiest woman alive."

"Don't count your chickens quite yet," Ray warned. "You still have to face Alice Frame."

"I'm sure once Sally knows that I'm her real grandmother, she'll want to come and live with me," Beatrice replied.

"Alice loves Sally, Mom. She's not going to give her up without a fight and you'd better prepare yourself for that."

But certainly Alice couldn't object if she knew that Sally wanted to be with her grandmother, Beatrice reasoned. So, the first thing she had to do then was to tell Sally the truth. When she called the Frame house to tell Alice that she was coming over, there was no answer. Beatrice looked at her watch. It was after eight o'clock. Where could Alice possibly have taken Sally at this hour of the night? she wondered.

After spending a restless night, Beatrice went over to see Jim Matthews the next morning.

"I've been trying to call Alice all night," she said in a panic. "There's been no answer. I'm really worried, Jim."

In the last month or so, Beatrice and Jim had become increasingly close. She knew that he'd been lonely since his wife, Mary, died. Beatrice was happy for his company, too. In fact, until all this business with Sally came up, Beatrice had actually entertained the idea of a serious relationship with Jim. Now, of course, that would be out of the question. It was awkward enough that he was Alice's father, but aside from that, Beatrice was going to have more than enough to do taking care of Sally to give any thought whatsoever to a social life of her own.

"Why don't I fix us a cup of tea," Jim offered, walking her into the living room.

"Jim, we've got to do something. Maybe we should call the police," she suggested, handing him her coat.

"I don't think that's necessary, Bea," he said softly.

Beatrice looked at him for a long moment. "You know where they are, don't you?"

"As a matter of fact I do," he replied.

Beatrice clutched her chest and felt the room beginning to spin as her legs started to give way. Jim helped her to a chair. All Beatrice could think of were those terrible cases she had heard of where one parent kidnaps their child to keep it away from the other parent. *Please God, don't let this be happening,* she prayed as Jim rushed over with a glass of water.

"Take it easy, Bea," she heard him say as she tried to sip the liquid.

"Alice has kidnapped Sally, hasn't she?" Beatrice cried, feeling a bit hysterical.

"Of course not!" Jim exclaimed, somewhat shocked that she could even entertain such a wild notion.

"Then why aren't they here?" Beatrice gasped, trying to catch her breath.

"Sally's school vacation is this week," Jim explained calmly. "Alice took her to the beach house in St. Croix for a few days."

"St. Croix! That's out of the country!" she exclaimed.

"Yes, I suppose it is. What difference does it make?" Jim asked innocently.

"Alice had no right to do that, Jim. She should have told me. After all, Sally is my granddaughter."

"I'll tell you what," Jim offered, attempting to calm

Beatrice down. "Why don't I call the beach house now and you can talk to Sally yourself?"

"Thank you, Jim. I would really appreciate that," Beatrice said, finishing her glass of water. As Jim dialed the number, Beatrice went over what she was going to say in her head. Alice had no right to treat her this way. Beatrice didn't care if Sally was in Timbuktu, she was going to know that she had a grandmother, and it was going to be now.

Jim handed her the phone. "Sally's on the line, Bea."

She took the phone slowly. "Would you mind, Jim? I'd like to talk to Sally in private." Jim knitted his brows uncomfortably. He was afraid Beatrice might be up to something, but there was really nothing he could do about it now. He picked up his newspaper and headed for the kitchen. Beatrice breathed a sigh of relief. This was the moment she had been waiting for.

"Hello, Sally?" she said somewhat tentatively.

"Hi, Mrs. Gordon, how are you? How is the weather in Bay City?" Sally's cheery voice asked.

"Well, it's pretty cold, honey," Beatrice replied.

"It's really beautiful here, almost ninety degrees. Can you believe it?"

"That's wonderful. Are you having a good time?"

"The best. Alice and I are going snorkeling today, and then tonight we're going to this really neat restaurant that has a view of the whole bay."

"That . . . sounds lovely, Sally," Beatrice stammered.

"Is there something else you wanted to tell me?" the little girl asked sweetly. Beatrice took a deep breath. How could she just blurt it out now, with Sally so many miles away and having such a good time? How could she tell her grandchild something so terribly important over the phone. The answer was, she couldn't. For now, she had to consider

Sally's welfare, and her granddaughter deserved to enjoy herself.

"Mrs. Gordon, are you still there?" the girl queried.

"Yes, Sally. Listen, honey, you have a good time, okay? I'll see you when you get back." Beatrice hung up the phone. She turned and saw that Jim was standing in the entrance.

"I wanted to tell her the truth, but I just couldn't ruin her vacation," she told him.

"I'm glad, Bea," Jim said, relieved. "There will be plenty of time for that when they get home."

Beatrice smiled weakly. "She sounded like she was having a wonderful time."

"Alice and Sally always have fun together," Jim said, smiling. Beatrice felt her heart sink. Maybe Raymond was right after all. There was no way that she could be the kind of mother to Sally that Alice was. Alice could offer the child advantages Beatrice couldn't begin to give her granddaughter. But even more than that, they seemed genuinely happy together. *That's all that really matters*, Beatrice thought.

She returned to the Corys' house feeling lonely and dejected. Rachel was quick to notice, and Beatrice was even quicker to pour out her heart.

"If you're worried about not being able to provide for Sally, don't be," Rachel reassured her. "Material comforts don't mean anything compared to the love you can give her," she said with deep conviction. No matter what anyone else thought of her for it, Rachel was convinced that Sally would be better off living with her grandmother —her family. It had nothing to do with the resentment she used to feel toward Alice. In fact, Rachel wished her former rival only the best. She just didn't happen to believe that Sally belonged with her.

"But where will we live?" Beatrice asked, her voice trembling.

"Right here," Rachel said.

"But my quarters are much too small for a child," Beatrice began.

"How would you feel about moving into the East Wing?" Rachel asked impulsively.

"Oh I couldn't, Mrs. Cory!"

"Of course you can. And you will," Rachel promised. "You just get that granddaughter of yours, and we'll see to it she has everything she needs."

"How generous of you, Rachel," Iris's voice sounded from the doorway. "Does Daddy know about this?"

After seeing John with Barbara Weaver at Sally's party, Liz Matthews had resolved to take matters into her own hands, whether the rest of the family approved or not. She walked out of the elevator on the seventh floor, and opened the door that was marked: "Randolph and Weaver, Attorneys-at-Law." She did not ring the bell first. Inside, Liz wandered around the waiting room. She checked her watch. It was just after closing time and John was guaranteed to still be in his office. But when she walked inside the plush, beige-carpeted room, there was no one there. In frustration, she looked through John's appointment book. He had an appointment with Judge Hawthorne at 5:30; she had just missed him. As she started to leave, Liz heard voices coming from down the hall. They were speaking very low, but as she inched her way along the corridor, she recognized one of the speakers as Marianne.

Huddled on the couch in Barbara's office, Marianne was already on her second box of tissues.

"I feel so ashamed, Barbara," the young woman said through her tears. "Do you think I did the right thing?"

Outside the door, Liz stopped to listen. Why on earth would Marianne be talking to Barbara Weaver about a personal matter? Liz couldn't help wondering.

"I can't answer that, Marianne," Barbara replied honestly. "I told you before, it's a very personal decision. What matters now is that you get on with your life."

"I'm trying, but it's so hard," Marianne sniffed. "I can't even look at my father anymore."

Liz arched her brows, full of curiosity. Obviously Marianne had done something she was ashamed of, and obviously John didn't know about it. But why would she be telling Barbara? Something was definitely not right, Liz decided as she continued to listen.

"I think your father has a right to know," Barbara was saying.

"You don't know what it would do to him, Barbara. You see, he thinks I'm perfect—that I can't do anything wrong."

"John is a grown man, Marianne. He'll understand. You seem to be forgetting that he loves you, and that by not telling him you're only making the situation worse. As it is now, he doesn't understand why you're acting the way you are."

Barbara's logic made sense to Marianne in her head, but in her heart she knew her father would never look at her the same way if he knew. She would never be his little girl again and the thought of that was more than she could bear. Maybe she was being selfish, or maybe just cowardly. But whatever the reason, she knew her father must never find out what she'd done.

"You're not going to tell Dad, are you?"

Barbara shook her head "It's not my place to."

Marianne breathed a sigh of relief. "I just need some time to get my head together."

"Don't take too long," Barbara advised. "If John finds out from someone else that you went to New York to have the abortion, just think how terrible it will make him feel."

Liz practically collapsed on the spot. An *abortion?* She could feel her heart racing. Marianne had had an abortion and her own family knew nothing about it. In fact, the only one who did seem to know anything was Barbara! Poor Pat, Liz thought. Both her husband and her daughter had betrayed her!

Later that evening John was nursing a brandy in front of the fire, feeling alone and thoroughly rejected, when the front door swung open. Pat was standing there with her suitcase.

"I had enough of Washington," she said as he hurried over to greet her. John hugged his wife tenderly.

"I'm so glad you're home," he said, his voice filled with emotion.

"I'm glad to be home," Pat replied, meaning every word.

For a while, it seemed to John that Pat was her old self again. Maybe the trip had done her some good after all. Pat felt the same way, at first. She'd had time to think, time away from all the pressures of home, and now she felt certain she could deal with them.

John was so happy that he broke open a bottle of champagne in their bedroom. "To us, my darling," he said, clinking his glass with hers.

"To us," Pat replied. John took her glass and placed it on the night table. He stroked her silky blond hair.

"You're so beautiful," he whispered, kissing her gently on the lips. Pat felt herself responding until his kisses became more urgent, more demanding. She felt his fingers quickly undoing the buttons of her blouse. "Oh, Pat," he whispered, his voice hoarse as he pulled her close and buried his face in her hair. Pat could feel her whole body stiffen. He picked her up and carried her to their bed. She watched with a mixture of intrest and dread as he undressed and came over to the bed.

"I've missed you so . . ." he sighed, kissing her passionately as his hands began to explore the rest of her body.

"John, please," Pat whispered, hoping he would stop. But he continued to caress her intimately.

"I want you so much," he said. Pat heard herself scream inside.

"No!" she cried as she bolted out of the bed, clutching her clothes to her chest.

John looked at her like a wounded animal. "Pat? What's wrong?"

Pat just stared at him, unable to say a word. Suddenly, she burst into tears and ran into the bathroom, locking the door behind her. She peered up at the mirror and saw her trembling reflection. Her face was flushed and her cheeks were streaked with black lines of mascara. "Oh God, what's happening to me?" she whispered.

Chapter Six
The Past Uncovered

Mac Cory was sitting behind his desk, leaning back in the soft, suede chair Rachel had given him for Christmas. He was almost finished reading a new manuscript when Iris tapped at his office door.

"Iris, what brings you over to the complex?" he asked as he got up and gave his daughter a hug.

"I was in town shopping and I thought I'd check up on you, Daddy," she replied, smiling sweetly. "Did Rachel tell you I stopped over the house yesterday?"

"It must have slipped her mind," Mac replied, unbothered.

Iris shrugged. "I suppose so, unless . . ."

"Unless what?" Mac asked, getting annoyed. He hated the way Iris beat around the bush sometimes. "If you have something to say, Iris, why not just say it?"

It was so easy to get a rise out of her father where Rachel was concerned, Iris reflected, pleased with herself. Obviously he wouldn't be so touchy every time her name was mentioned if he wasn't secretly embarrassed by her complete lack of breeding and social grace. So it wasn't that she was being a troublemaker, Iris figured. She merely cared about her father. And she was determined to show him the error he'd made in marrying that woman, in living color.

"Well, I did happen to walk in on something, but maybe I shouldn't say anything . . . besides, you probably know already, otherwise Rachel would have never made the offer. . . ." Iris waited for Mac's reaction, which was entirely predictable.

"What offer? Will you please tell me what you're talking about?" he snapped, his blood pressure starting to rise.

"I'm talking about Beatrice and Sally moving into the East Wing," Iris cooed.

"That's absurd!"

"Well, yes, that's what I thought until I heard Rachel invite Beatrice to do just that once she won the custody suit against Alice."

Mac frowned. "It's that again, is it? Rachel knows how much I dislike the thought of her upsetting Alice."

"I told you Rachel was determined to ruin Alice's life, Daddy, but you wouldn't believe me. But this proves it. I mean, if Beatrice doesn't have a proper place to live, she couldn't possibly be awarded custody, could she?"

Much as he hated to admit it, Mac was painfully aware that his wife had a terrible habit of meddling in other people's lives. He knew she was only trying to do what she thought was right, but the point was that the custody battle over Sally Spenser was none of her affair. This meddling could not be allowed to continue, Mac thought. Rachel would either have to learn to mind her own business, or there was bound to be trouble between them.

"I hope you're not angry with me for telling you, Daddy," Iris purred, tilting her head innocently.

"No, Iris, I'm glad you said something. I'm not going to allow Rachel to interfere in Alice's life anymore."

"Well, of course you can try, but—"

Mac cut her off. "That'll be enough, Iris. I know it gives you pleasure to find fault with Rachel. . . ."

"That's not true, I'm only concerned about you, Daddy!" she protested.

He looked at his daughter fondly. "Nevertheless, I don't want you to see this as an open invitation to insult Rachel, is that clear?"

"Yes, Daddy," Iris replied, gloating inwardly. It was only a matter of time. Once Mac started socializing with Tracey DeWitt again, he'd realize what a mistake he'd made in marrying Rachel. And fortunately for Iris, Tracey was due back in town very soon. Iris had plotted to reunite Mac with his old flame several weeks ago, but her plans were interrupted when Tracey had gone back to Washington for the holidays. But she'd be back soon enough, and this time Iris would make sure she stayed for good.

Rachel was working on her newest clay model in the studio when Mac arrived.

"Mac," she cried, smiling happily, "I didn't expect you home for lunch."

"I want to know what's going on with you and Alice, Rachel," Mac demanded.

"I don't know what you mean."

"I don't want you to involve yourself in Alice Frame's affairs, particularly Sally's adoption."

"I'm not!" she protested, feeling terrible for angering Mac. "Not exactly . . ."

"Then why did you invite Beatrice to move into the East Wing if she wins custody of Sally?" Mac bellowed, his face growing red with rage.

Rachel clenched her teeth. "I see Iris has been talking to you again," she said, throwing down the clay mold angrily. Mac grabbed her wrist.

"That's not the point, Rachel, and you know it!"

"Don't you see, she'll do anything she can to make trouble between us, Mac."

"You're doing a pretty good job of that all by yourself,"

Mac insisted. "When were you going to tell me about Beatrice and Sally? Presumably before they took over part of our home?"

"I was only offering the woman a place to stay. And I thought you, of all people, would understand. Beatrice needs us."

"That's beside the point!" Mac railed, becoming increasingly frustrated. "Your offer may have been just the encouragement Beatrice needed to fight Alice for custody of Sally." Looking at his lovely wife, Mac softened. "Oh, Rachel . . ."

Rachel put her hands on her hips and looked at her husband. "Just because I'm married to you, Mac, it doesn't mean I don't have a right to my own opinions and beliefs. And I happen to believe that Beatrice should have custody of Sally if she wants it!"

"But it's not your affair, Rachel. I'm telling you for the last time to stay out of it!"

"But, Mac . . ." Before Rachel could say more, he had left the room. A few seconds later, she heard the front door slam shut. Rachel curled her hands tightly into fists.

"Damn Iris. Damn her to hell!"

At the end of the week, Jim Matthews met Alice and Sally at the airport. They were both bubbling over about the wonderful time they'd had in St. Croix, and Sally was particularly pleased about a plaque she had earned after successfully completing her snorkeling classes. Their exuberance made it even more difficult than it would normally have been to tell Alice the news.

"Something's wrong, isn't it, Dad?" she asked when they were finally home and Sally was upstairs in her bedroom unpacking.

"I'm afraid we've got some trouble, honey," Jim advised, not knowing quite how to break the news. But somehow, Alice already knew.

"It's about Sally, isn't it," she said, lowering her voice almost to a whisper.

"Yes, it is."

Jim walked her over to the couch and they sat down. He looked into his younger daughter's anxiety-filled eyes, and thought he couldn't bear to add to their pain. He took her hands in his and squeezed them reassuringly.

"Go on, Dad, you can tell me. Honest," Alice encouraged.

"Beatrice has filed a custody suit of her own."

Alice put her hand over her mouth in shock. "Oh, no!" she gasped, looking at her father with searching eyes. "How could she do that? She knows how much Sally means to me?"

Jim took his daughter in his arms. "I think Beatrice is just confused right now, Alice. I'm sure she'll come to her senses before long."

Alice looked at her father a moment. Panic began to show in her troubled eyes. "What if she doesn't? You know what that means, don't you, Dad; it means a court fight."

"I'm sure it won't come to that. And if it does I'll talk to Beatrice myself."

"It won't do any good. She wouldn't have gone this far if she didn't intend to stick to her guns." Alice sighed. Then her expression became firm. "Well I won't give Sally up—not to Beatrice, not to anyone!" Alice burst into tears and ran out of the room. Jim picked up the snorkeling plaque Sally had left on the coffee table. There was no way he would allow Beatrice Gordon to separate Alice and Sally. No way in the world!

When Ray Gordon heard that Alice was back in town, he didn't waste any time before giving her a call and inviting her out to lunch. Alice, however, was not very receptive. Shell-shocked from the news about Beatrice's custody suit, she informed Ray that it probably wasn't a good idea for them to spend time together. After all, the battle lines were now drawn and it wouldn't have been appropriate for them to cross over as if nothing were wrong.

"How about a short truce?" Ray persisted. "I think Tall Boys qualifies as neutral territory, don't you?"

Alice finally relented, and later that day the two met for lunch. Alice tried not to let her resentment show as she stared across the table at Ray, but it was impossible. First he had come to Bay City threatening to take Sally away from her, and now his mother had actually begun custody proceedings. How could she not resent him?

"I know you probably don't have the warmest feelings for me at the moment," he began tentatively.

Alice sipped her white wine. "You're right, I don't."

"Look, if it's any consolation, I'm against what my mother's doing."

"I'm sorry, but it isn't." There was a long, awkward silence between them as Alice sat rigidly in her chair, glaring at him.

"Alice, I'm not the enemy," he finally said, softly.

"Oh, is that why you're allowing this to happen?"

"I can't control what my mother does."

"That's a pretty feeble excuse for breaking up a family, don't you think. Or maybe it didn't occur to you or your mother that that's what Sally and I are; a family," Alice challenged, tears beginning to well in her eyes.

"I realized that at Sally's birthday party; that's why I decided not to press the custody issue myself. More than that, I don't think my mother should get Sally either."

Alice stared at Ray with a confused look. "I don't understand what you're trying to say."

"I'm saying that my mother is the last person who should be awarded custody of that little girl," Ray replied with candor.

No matter how Ray tried to see the issue, no matter

how he twisted and turned the facts, one glaring truth remained: Beatrice had been a stifling, over-protective, overly strict mother with Jenny. She had, unintentional though it may have been, pushed his younger sister right out the front door and inadvertantly paved the way for the tragic turn her life was to take. Even with his sons in California, Beatrice had behaved the same way; she was always at them for one reason or another, never allowing them the freedom to develop on their own.

During the last week or so in Bay City, he had seen no indication that Beatrice had changed her ways, or even could have if she'd wanted to. In all probability, she wasn't even aware of her problem. Unfortunately, he had let her con him into at least tacit agreement with her plan to sue for custody. All of her begging and pleading over dinner that evening had been a bit more than he could take. But now, seeing Alice sitting across from him, there wasn't a doubt in his mind that she should be the one to adopt Sally. And he would do whatever he could to facilitate the matter. If his mother was hurt by that, then so be it. He had to follow his conscience.

"Are you saying you're going to help me?" Alice asked, incredulous.

"Yes," Ray replied, earnestly. "I'm going to talk to my mother and if that doesn't work, then we'll see where we should go from there."

Alice reached across the table and put her hand over his. "I can't tell you what this means to me," she said through tear-filled eyes. "I love Sally so much. I can't even imagine what my life would be like without her. She's been all I have since my husband died."

Ray had heard about Steve Frame's disappearance and presumed death from Beatrice. "You must have loved him very much," he commented.

"Steven was my world," Alice whispered, the love she still felt for him apparent in her voice.

"It's a very rare thing to share a love like that. I envy you, Alice."

Alice smiled warmly. Somehow, from the moment they had dashed out in the snow to pick up Sally's birthday cake together, Alice had known that Raymond was a very special person. He was warm and compassionate, and in that way he most reminded her of Steven. But although she felt drawn to him, Alice had to remind herself that Raymond was a married man and she was still exceedingly vulnerable emotionally.

"You must miss your wife and children very much," Alice finally said.

"I miss the boys; they're great kids. Olive is another matter."

"I'm sorry. I didn't mean to pry," Alice apologized.

"You didn't. The truth is, things aren't very good between my wife and me. They haven't been for a long time."

"I'm sorry, Raymond. You're a nice man." Alice got up from the table, realizing that if she didn't leave, the conversation could take a turn that neither of them was prepared for. "Thank you for lunch."

"Can I drive you home?" he asked, hoping for the chance to spend even a little more time with her.

"No, thank you. I've got my car," she replied, starting to leave. Ray caught her by the wrist. For a moment, they held each other's gaze and Alice began to feel as if she were drowning in his dark brown eyes.

"I'll call you . . . about Sally," he said, trying to cover his true feelings.

"Please do," Alice said with a smile. They stood staring at each other for a moment before Ray realized he was still holding on to her wrist. He laughed nervously and released his grip.

"Maybe we can have dinner one evening?"

"That would be nice," Alice replied. He watched as she

headed toward the door, her long, blond hair swinging as she walked away. Ray could barely catch his breath. Alice Frame looked like an angel.

Although the wind was whipping along Sycamore Street, Liz Matthews just rolled up the fur collar on her black woolen coat and continued to watch John's building from across the street. Any minute now, Barbara would be leaving for the day, and then Liz would have her chance to speak with John alone. She had tried phoning Pat several times, but each time they spoke, her niece sounded troubled and found some excuse to get off the phone. Something had to be done, and her only alternative was to speak to John.

In her heart, Liz was firmly convinced that Barbara was the cause of all the troubles in the Randolph family, particularly after she overheard the conversation between her and Marianne. To think that her great-niece had confided in a stranger and not in her own family! And worse, Marianne had obviously been pushed into the abortion by that horrible woman. Well, Liz told herself, John was going to know the kind of a woman Barbara was once and for all.

It was after six o'clock, and Liz had been standing on the blustry corner for nearly forty-five minutes when she saw Barbara leave the building and head for the parking lot. Losing no time, Liz sprinted across the icy street and took the elevator up to John's office. As usual, he was still at his desk, poring over some briefs. *No wonder Pat is so miserable*, Liz reflected. *John never spends any time at home!*

John, however, had a different point of view entirely. Pat didn't seem to want him at home. Since that night she had bolted out of their bed when he'd tried to make love to her, John had been nursing his wounded pride.

"Liz," he said, looking up from his paperwork at the sound of someone entering. "What are you doing here?"

Liz took off her coat and sat down. Her expression was grave, as it usually was when she wanted to discuss family matters. "John . . . there's something I think you should know," she began tentatively.

"This sounds pretty serious, Liz," he remarked in a distracted tone.

"It's about Barbara Weaver."

John slapped the papers down on his desk with a thud. "I know you don't like Barbara—it's nothing new—but I am not going to sit here and listen to gossip about a friend!"

"Even if that so-called friend has betrayed you?"

John got up and circled her like a tiger ready to pounce. "Say what you've got to say, Liz, and then get out of here," John snapped angrily.

"Why is it that you turn into a brick wall every time that woman's name is mentioned?" Liz asked, exasperated.

"I don't have to listen to this," John replied, standing up and starting to pull on his coat. Liz stopped him.

"Oh yes you do, John. You do if you care a fig about Marianne and Pat."

John turned, suddenly concerned. "What does Barbara have to do with them?"

Liz took a deep breath. Obviously John didn't know anything about Marianne's abortion. Barbara must have arranged the whole thing, realizing that when it all came out it would create havoc in the family and then she would have John all to herself.

"Well, Liz? Are you going to back up your accusations or do we end this discussion here and now?"

She couldn't believe the hostility in his voice. Now she was sure her suspicions were correct. If John wasn't involved with his law partner, why would he try to defend her so?

"It's about Marianne's trip to New York," she began slowly. "Do you know why she went?"

Now John was really interested; his daughter's holiday departure had continued to disturb him. "To visit with Glenda and her family," John replied.

Liz shook her head sadly. "I'm afraid you've been lied to, John. But it wasn't Marianne's fault. Barbara is the one who pushed her into this!"

"Into what? You're not making any sense, Liz!" John said, raising his voice in frustration.

"Do you remember the horrible young man Marianne was involved with?"

"Chris? He left town, for heaven's sake. That's all over with, thank heaven," John replied.

"I'm afraid it's not. You see, Marianne got pregnant." Liz watched the shock register on John's face as he stared at her in disbelief.

"That's impossible. . . ." His voice trailed off.

"It's the truth. Apparently, when Marianne found out, she talked it over with Barbara."

"That's ridiculous. Why would she tell Barbara and not her mother or me?"

Liz shrugged. "I don't know. But I do know that it was your partner who convinced her to go to New York and have an abortion!" Liz pronounced dramatically. She thought for a moment that John was going to go right through the roof. His face turned a deathly shade of white as he leveled her with an incredulous glare.

"An abortion?"

"That was my reaction, too."

"No, it can't be!" he said, pacing the room like a caged animal. "There's got to be some other explanation."

"I heard them talking, John. It's true. If you don't believe me, ask Barbara and then you'll see that I was right about her all along. She's trying to ruin your family. She's moving in on you, John, just like Bernice Kline did!"

John turned on her. "Get out!" he yelled.

93

"John, I'm only telling you the truth!" Liz protested as he came closer.

"Get out, I said. And don't ever come back here again!"

That night, John did not go home. He stayed in his office until the next morning, staring vacantly into space. When Barbara came in, she found him, unshaven and slumped over his desk in a troubled sleep.

"John, John wake up," she said softly, shaking him.

He awakened with a start and stared at Barbara, trying to focus. "You!" he hissed.

Barbara recoiled, frightened. "What is it, John? Tell me what's wrong?"

He staggered out of his chair, stiff from sitting in one position all night. "I trusted you," he said, staring at her. "How could you do such a thing?" He grabbed her by the shoulders and shook her until Barbara thought she would faint.

"Please, John, stop it! I don't know what you're talking about!" Finally, he released her. Barbara straightened her blouse and fought to regain her composure. "Now, would you please tell me what this is all about," she said.

"Why did you convince Marianne to have an abortion?" he asked, his voice accusing.

"I didn't," Barbara protested. "Who told you such a terrible lie?"

"You knew all about it, didn't you?" he asked, cut to the quick.

"Oh, John, I told Marianne this would happen. I begged her to go to you and tell you the truth."

John shook his head in disbelief. It was like a nightmare. But finally, the events of the last few weeks were beginning to make some kind of sense. "Are you saying that Marianne confided in you?"

Barbara was silent for a long time. Then she said,

SUSPICIONS

"Marianne came to me and told me she was pregnant and wanted to get an abortion. I advised her against it, at least until after she'd discussed it with you and Pat. She promised she would, and begged me to keep her confidence. The next thing I heard, she'd already had the abortion." She sighed. "I'm sorry, John."

He covered his face with his hands and began to cry. Barbara felt her heart being wrenched in two. Nothing seemed more natural to her just then than to put her arm around her partner. "I'm so very sorry, John," she continued to whisper as he buried his head in her breast.

It was a long time before he regained his composure. He looked at his partner, embarrassed. "Forgive me. I should have known better than to believe you could have had any hand in this business."

Barbara touched his arm gently. "It's all right."

"I just don't understand why Marianne couldn't come to me. Or if not me, certainly her mother." Barbara tried to avert his eyes, but John noticed it immediately. "Did Pat know about this?" he asked, suddenly sure she was covering something. Barbara looked up at him, but said nothing.

Mac was unusually quiet at the breakfast table, burying himself in the morning paper. Rachel sat opposite him, pushing her scrambled eggs around on her plate. Finally she put her fork down and stared at her husband.

"How much longer are you going to give me the silent treatment," she asked.

Mac put down his paper. "I'm not giving you the silent treatment. I'm just trying to read the paper."

"You're still mad because I invited Beatrice and Sally to live here, aren't you?"

"I'm not mad, but I am rather surprised you'd do a thing like that without discussing it with me."

"There wasn't time. I told you, it all happened so fast."

95

"And I told you to stay out of it from the beginning. That still holds. I don't want to hear anything else about Beatrice's problems with Alice." He got up from the table and picked up his briefcase. "I'll be home for dinner."

Rachel couldn't stand it when Mac was disappointed in her. She'd only offered Beatrice a place to bring Sally, because she had compassion for the woman. And of course, none of this would have even happened if Iris hadn't gone to Mac. Rachel would have had time to explain the situation to him in her own way, and she was certain Mac's attitude would have been completely different.

Suddenly, the loud ringing of the phone interrupted her thoughts. Glumly, Rachel reached over to the wall and answered it.

"Hello?"

"Rachel. Hello, dear, this is Iris."

Rachel arched her brow. If ever anyone had a sense of bad timing, it was Iris! If she could have, Rachel would have reached through the phone and grabbed her by her highly-perfumed neck. "What do you want, Iris?"

"That's not a very nice greeting, dear."

"I asked what you wanted, Iris."

"Actually, I wanted to speak with Daddy. Is he still there?"

"You know he leaves for the office before now."

"Well then, perhaps you can give him a message for me?"

"Fine, what's the message?" Rachel snapped, tapping her foot impatiently on the floor.

"Just tell him his old friend is back in town. . . ."

"Who?" Rachel asked.

"Tracey DeWitt, dear. You didn't think she had left for good, did you?" Iris laughed and hung up before Rachel could respond.

Soaps & Serials™ Fans!

★ Order the *Soaps & Serials*™ books you have missed in this series.

★ Collect other *Soaps & Serials*™ series from their very beginnings.

★ Give *Soaps & Serials*™ series as gifts to other fans.

...see other side for ordering information

Soaps & Serials™
From Pioneer Communications Network, Inc.

You can now order previous titles of *Soaps & Serials*™ Books by mail!

Just complete the order form, detach, and send together with your check or money order payable to:

Soaps & Serials™
120 Brighton Road, Box 5201
Clifton, NJ 07015-5201

- - - - - - - - - - - - - - - - - - -

Please <u>circle</u> the book #'s you wish to order:

The Young and The Restless	1	2	3	4	5	6	7	8	9
Days of Our Lives	1	2	3	4	5	6	7	8	9
Guiding Light	1	2	3	4	5	6	7	8	9
Another World	1	2	3	4	5	6	7	8	9
As The World Turns	1	2	3	4	5	6	7	8	9
Dallas™	1	2	3	4	5	6	7	8	9
Knots Landing™	1	2	3	4	5	6	7	8	9
Capitol™	1	2	3	4	NOT AVAILABLE				

Each book is $2.50 ($3.50 in Canada).

Total number of books
circled _____ × price above = $ _____

Sales tax (CT and NY residents only) $ _____

Shipping and Handling $ _____ .95

Total payment enclosed $ _____
(check or money orders only)

Name _____

Address _____ Apt# _____

City _____

State _____ Zip _____

Telephone (_____) _____
Area code

AW 9

Chapter Seven
A Change Of Heart

It was common knowledge in Washington circles that stunning socialite Tracey DeWitt and her husband, millionaire Claude DeWitt, were no longer a couple. Though Claude had been rather generous in providing for his wife's comforts, she was through putting up with his philanderings. She longed for a husband who would love and honor her. It was with precisely that in mind that she had taken her old friend Iris up on her invitation to visit with her in Bay City for a few weeks.

Tracey and Iris were sipping mid-morning tea in the solarium when Robert entered with his briefcase. Iris immediately jumped up and slid her arms around her husband's waist. After the incident with Scott Bradley, she feared she had pushed Robert too far. He hadn't come to her room at night, or even really spoken to her, for days and Iris was beginning to panic. How would it look if Robert were to walk out on her? And her intuition told her in exactly whose direction he would walk if he did leave: Clarice Hobson's. There was no way Iris Carrington would lose her husband to a waitress!

"Darling, won't you try to come home early tonight?" she asked, toying with his tie.

"I may have a meeting, Iris," Robert answered curtly.

"I have something special planned," she teased.

"What, another dinner with Scott Bradley? Or were you planning to invite Beatrice Gordon this time?"

"Oh, Robert, do stop being so cross." Iris pouted. "I told you I was sorry about all that."

"Did you? It must have slipped my mind!" He closed his briefcase and looked over at Tracey. "Have a nice day, Tracey."

"Thank you. I intend to."

Iris blocked her husband's path, standing there like a petulant child with her face raised for a kiss. Robert kissed her brusquely on the cheek. "Try to be good, Iris." He left, and Iris stamped her small foot on the hardwood floor in frustration.

"Trouble in paradise, darling?" Tracey asked.

Iris waved it off. "Not a bit. I can handle Robert."

"I'm sure you can. You could handle just about anything," Tracey said with a laugh, plunking a sugar cube into her tea.

"I have a wonderful idea, Tracey," Iris said, her eyes brightening. "Why don't you go over to the complex and surprise Daddy for lunch?"

"I don't know. Don't you think that's rather pushy?"

"Not at all. Daddy likes women who take charge," Iris encouraged her friend.

Tracey needed very little encouragement. Wearing the opera-length mink coat Claude had given her for her last birthday, Tracey appeared at Mac's office, conveniently just after noon.

Mac greeted her with enthusiasm. "This is a surprise," he exclaimed, giving her a friendly hug.

"I told you I was going to show up at your office one of these days." She flashed him a dazzling smile. Her flaming red hair flowed generously over her collar as Mac looked at her appreciatively.

"I'm going to take you out to lunch," he insisted.

"Oh, I wouldn't want to interfere with your plans," she said, intending to do just that.

"Don't be silly," Mac replied. "I was just going to go back to the house. I'll just call Rachel and tell her not to expect me until dinner."

Tracey lifted an eyebrow. Maybe Iris was right about the state of Mac's marriage all along. She watched her former lover as he made his excuses to Rachel over the phone, never once mentioning that he was lunching with her. Yes, she thought, he was still a fine figure of a man. He was distinguished-looking with his salt-and-pepper-gray hair and his small, well-trimmed mustache. And they'd had quite a time together, she recalled. It was the summer she'd spent in Paris before she met Claude and long before there was ever a Rachel to contend with. She and Mac had painted the town red, drinking champagne and dancing their way from the Club Lido to the Moulin Rouge, then topping it all with a late night supper at Maxim's. Ah, what a summer that had been. What she didn't quite understand or even remember was how she could have let Mac Cory get away. Well, perhaps she was being given a second chance, she thought as he walked over and took her arm.

"We're all set," he said, filled with the same energy of their Paris summer so long ago. This was definitely going to be an interesting lunch, Tracey decided.

The afternoon was made far more interesting by the fact that Rachel decided to call her mother on the spur of the moment and treat her to lunch. As they settled into their table at Tall Boys, Ada's eyes practically popped out of their sockets. She tried not to let on that anything was wrong, but her daughter had a keen eye for trouble.

"Ma, what on earth are you staring at?" Rachel inquired.

She knew it was totally out of character for her mother to be shocked by anything.

"It's nothing," Ada tried to cover, moving the menu up in front of her face.

Rachel turned around to see what had caused such a stir. It only took a few seconds for her glance to fall on a corner table across the room where her husband was sitting and laughing with one of the most beautiful-looking women she had ever seen.

"She's probably one of those new writers Cory Publishing is always signing up," Ada offered.

"Mac said he was having a business lunch," Rachel replied, feeling her blood pressure rise.

"Now don't go getting all worked up. Remember the baby. Like I said, she's probably one of those romance novelists. You know how done up they always get."

"That's no romance writer," Rachel snapped as she started up from her seat, "that's Tracey DeWitt."

Ada stopped her. "Where do you think you're going?"

"I'm going to find out what's going on," Rachel told her.

"Sit down," Ada ordered her daughter. "You are not going to go over there and make a scene like some jealous wife."

Rachel was livid. "What am I supposed to do? Just sit here and enjoy a nice lunch while my husband is wining and dining that woman over there?"

"Look, Rachel, you're Mrs. Mackenzie Cory now. You have a position in this community to uphold. If you have something to say to Mac, you'll do it in the privacy of your own home. Is that clear?"

Rachel stared back at her mother. She didn't like it one bit, but she also knew Ada was right. Besides, what if it really was a business lunch and she went flying over there like a jealous wife? Mac might think she was acting impulsively, like a child, and she certainly didn't want to disappoint him or worse, cause him any embarrassment. For the time being, she decided to grin, bear it, and order a spinach salad.

Later that afternoon, Iris called the Cory house.

"I just wondered if Tracey was still with Mac?" she asked Rachel, playing the perfect innocent.

"Tracey?" Rachel inquired, her blood beginning to boil all over again.

"Why, yes, dear. We had dinner plans, but she hasn't come back from the complex yet and it's been hours. I suppose Daddy took her out to lunch, but they must certainly be finished by now."

Rachel could barely contain her anger. "I'll give Mac your message, Iris."

"You're not angry, are you? I mean, I'm quite sure there's nothing to be concerned about. Tracey and Daddy are just friends now," Iris said, baiting her.

"I'm well aware of that."

"They *were* the toast of Paris in the old days . . . But I'm sure Daddy told you all about that. Well, if you see Tracey before I do, tell her to hurry back." Iris hung up the phone. She couldn't help laughing aloud. It was so easy to get to Rachel. In a way, that almost spoiled the fun.

When Mac came home for dinner that evening, Rachel was so angry she was ready to burst. Still, she decided to give him the benefit of the doubt and see if he would willingly tell her about his lunch date. If he did, she had nothing to worry about. If not, it was time to take action.

"How did your lunch meeting go?" Rachel asked as she mixed him a martini.

"Actually, it was more of a social visit than a meeting," he admitted freely.

"Oh?"

"Tracey DeWitt stopped by the complex. She's interested in doing a photography book for us," he explained.

"That's nice," Rachel replied casually.

"I felt I had to take her to lunch. She just showed up unexpectedly. I'm sorry, darling."

Instantly, Rachel felt all of the pent-up anger drain out of her. Why she continued to be insecure about her relationship with Mac was beyond her. "As long as you come home to me at night, I don't care if you take Elizabeth Taylor out to lunch," she said with a laugh, half-meaning it as she put her arms around his neck.

"I'm sure Liz will be thrilled to hear that," Mac teased back.

"I don't know, maybe I should be jealous. I know Tracey is a real beauty."

"You're the only girl for me and you know it!" Mac replied.

"Come on. I'll bet you don't think I'm half as interesting or beautiful as Tracey DeWitt," Rachel probed, smiling sweetly.

"Tracey's all right. But she can't hold a candle to my Rachel," Mac said, kissing his wife. Rachel felt like a huge weight had been lifted from her shoulders. For a split second, when she saw Mac and Tracey together, she thought she might be losing him and if that had happened, she would have wanted to die.

As for Iris, Rachel was not about to let her off easily this time. She had definitely made up her mind to tell Mac about Iris's part in keeping it from Robert that he was the father of Clarice's baby. But not tonight. Tonight she wanted Mac, happy, contented and all to herself.

It had taken Alice awhile to get herself together after learning of Beatrice's custody petition. She knew her only real hope was to talk Beatrice out of pursuing the matter. She also believed that if she appealed to the woman's reason, along with her better nature, Beatrice would have to see the folly of her actions. After all, Alice had always treated Beatrice as a friend. She had opened her home to Beatrice, trusting her completely with Sally. The child had also grown rather fond of her babysitter. Telling Sally that Beatrice was her real grandmother would have only enhanced that relationship, not destroyed it. All Alice had to do was convince Beatrice of that. She had no wish to keep Sally from her grandmother. On the contrary, Alice wanted to encourage them to become as close as possible.

Beatrice, however, did not seem terribly receptive when she arrived at Alice's home. The atmosphere was strained, to put it mildly. Moreover, Beatrice was still reeling from the shock of Alice spiriting Sally off to St. Croix without telling her. She certainly was in no mood to have Alice try to talk her out of getting custody of her own granddaughter.

"I don't think there's very much we can say to each other, Alice," Beatrice began, keeping her distance.

"Sally means a lot to both of us, Beatrice. Don't you think we owe it to her to try and talk this out?"

"I want my granddaughter, Alice. Nothing you can say is going to change that."

Alice started to panic. She had a whole speech prepared, but now Beatrice had knocked every word of it right out of her head. There was only one thought in her mind now: somehow she had to convince Beatrice to drop the suit before Sally found out and was put smack in the middle of all the ugliness.

"I love Sally, Beatrice. I know you know that. She means everything to me. She couldn't mean any more if she were my natural daughter."

"I know you do, Alice, but I'm her own flesh and blood. Sally is all I have left of my beautiful Jenny," Beatrice said with deep conviction.

"I know that. And I'm sure you remember how you felt the day you lost your daughter . . ."

Beatrice turned away. The memory was so painful to

recall, but suddenly it came flooding back like a tidal wave. First the screams, then the panic, the running from one room to the next and then the discovery—an empty closet and a note:

> Dear Mama,
>   I don't want to hurt you, but I just can't take your being mad at me anymore. Billy and I are going to get married. I'm sorry you don't approve, but you never approve of anything I do.
>
>   Good-bye, Jenny

Beatrice tried to shake the memory from her mind. There were two, maybe three phone calls after that. Then she'd lost contact with her daughter completely. When she learned of the car accident, she had been devastated, completely unaware that her Jenny had left a baby behind. Why couldn't her own daughter have told her she was pregnant? But deep down, Beatrice already knew the answer.

Tears sprang into Beatrice's eyes. "You don't understand, Alice. I need to be with Sally. I owe it to Jennifer," she said, her voice beginning to crack.

"I don't want to take her away from you. I want us to be a family together," Alice insisted. "I want Sally to have a grandmother like other kids."

"She doesn't even know I am her grandmother," Beatrice protested. "You took her off to St. Croix without telling me . . ."

"I apologize," Alice began, genuinely sorry. "I just thought it would be good for the both of us to get away and have some fun before we had to face this terrible battle. You can understand that, can't you? I wanted Sally to enjoy herself in the sun for a few days." Alice searched the older woman's face. "I just don't want her to be hurt, Beatrice."

"Do you think I do?" Beatrice cried.

"No, I don't. I believe that in your heart you want what's best for Sally, and I'm even going to let you be the judge."

"What do you mean?" Beatrice asked, confused.

"I thought you might like to spend some time alone with Sally."

Beatrice stared at Alice in semi-shock. "You'll let me talk to Sally alone?"

"I always have before, why should it be any different now?" Alice asked. "All I want you to do is ask yourself if she's happy here. If your answer is yes, then I know in my heart you'll do what's right. If you really love her, I know you won't take my little girl away from me!"

Alice left the room and Beatrice felt suddenly numb. There was no question that Alice Frame was a fine young woman. Beatrice had often remarked to people what a wonderful mother she was, how happy she and Sally were together. It was just that now Beatrice couldn't quite get past the reality that Sally was Jenny's daughter. What if she were to drop her suit and Alice had a change of heart? She could easily forbid her to see her granddaughter. She could even move away and then Beatrice would have lost her baby for a second time!

Beatrice's head was spinning when Sally flew merrily into the living room and plopped down right next to her.

Sally gave her a hug. "Hi, Mrs. Gordon. Alice said you wanted to talk to me?"

Beatrice put her arm around her granddaughter and smiled. "I sure did. I thought you might want to tell me about your trip."

"Oh, it was great!" Sally exclaimed. "We did all sorts of terrific things. We even went deep sea fishing one day."

"Did you catch anything?"

"No, but it was still fun," Sally told her.

"My little girl used to love to go fishing, too," Beatrice recalled with fondness.

"I didn't know you had a little girl." Sally looked up at Beatrice with sudden interest.

"Well, she wouldn't be little anymore," Beatrice explained. "Jenny would be about Alice's age."

"Where is she now?"

Beatrice smiled sadly. "She's not with me anymore. Jennifer died a long time ago."

Sally's usually bright face seemed to darken. "That's too bad. My mom died, too. Right after I was born. Sometimes I wonder what she was like; you know, what she looked like and stuff like that."

"I'll bet she was every bit as pretty as you."

"I wish I had a picture or something," Sally said. "It's kind of weird not knowing what your own mother looked like."

"I'll bet you wish she was with you right now," Beatrice commented.

Sally shrugged. "Well, Alice is like my real mom. I love her so much. She always tells me that I should be extra proud because I have two moms. I guess if my real mom was here, I'd love her, too, but I could never leave Alice."

That night, Beatrice couldn't sleep. All she could think of was Sally and how much the child loved Alice. If she were to take her away from the Frame house, she might never forgive her. In fact, she might even grow to resent her as much as Jenny had in the end. Suddenly, Beatrice remembered the night her daughter ran away. They'd had a terrible argument. Jenny had called her the worst mother in the world.

"You don't care about me at all!" Jenny had railed. "All you want to do is control my life and make me into a carbon copy of you!"

"That's not true, Jenny," Beatrice had tried to reason. "I only want what's best for you, can't you see that?"

"How do you know what's best? You never let me go anywhere. You won't let me have friends. You wouldn't even let me go to the prom! What kind of a mother wouldn't let her daughter go to her own prom?" Jenny yelled, tears streaming down her face.

"I told you, I don't want you hanging out with that bad crowd," Beatrice tried to explain.

"They happen to be my friends, but I guess that doesn't mean anything to you. Nothing that matters to me means anything to you does it?"

"Of course it does. Baby, I love you!" Beatrice had cried.

"Would you just listen to yourself? I'm seventeen years old, I'm not your baby anymore."

"You'll always be my baby, Jenny."

Jenny shook her head in complete frustration. "It's impossible. You'll never understand. You don't care what I feel. You don't even know the first thing about me."

"You're my beautiful little girl, and I'll love you till the day I die!"

Jenny looked at her mother for a long time. Nothing she said now mattered. Beatrice hadn't heard any of her arguments, not really, not enough to make a difference.

"I do love you, Jenny," Beatrice had whispered at last.

"I know you do. You just have a lousy way of showing it."

Beatrice Gordon leaned back in her rocking chair. Those were the last words her daughter had said to her. The next morning, all her clothes were gone, and she was out of Beatrice's life forever. Maybe she had loved her daughter too much, Beatrice thought. And maybe Jenny was right. She just had a lousy way of showing it.

After a long and sleepless night, Beatrice called her son the next morning. "I spoke to Alice yesterday," she began slowly, trying to collect her own thoughts.

"You two didn't get into an argument, did you?" Ray asked, concerned.

"No, it was very civilized," Beatrice explained. "Alice told me why she wanted Sally, and I told her how I felt."

"Then what?" Ray asked, fearing they had once again reached a stalemate.

Beatrice sighed wearily. "I couldn't help thinking about Jennifer last night," she said, clearly agitated.

"Are you all right, Mom?" Ray asked, worried that she might be heading for another depression like the one she experienced after Jenny left home.

"I'm not cracking up, if that's what you're worried about." Beatrice let out a short laugh.

"I didn't mean that, Mom. It's just that you sound upset."

It had taken months to coax her out of her depression after Jenny left home. Then, when they got the news of Jenny's death several years later, it was the same thing all over again. Beatrice blamed herself for everything that had happened. In part, she was surely responsible for her daughter's fate, but Beatrice had stretched it way out of proportion. She had made up her mind to spend the rest of her life atoning for the tragedy. That she was now in such a tense situation over Sally wasn't much help. In fact, Ray feared it might just push his mother over the edge.

"I don't know what to do, Raymond," she said, her voice filled with pain and confusion.

"Exactly what happened between you and Alice?" he asked, trying to get his mother to calm down and explain herself.

"She let me speak to Sally," Beatrice said in a rush. Then she took a deep breath and continued. "It was awful. Oh, Raymond, Sally loves Alice so much. She might hate me if I try to separate them and then she might run away from me just like Jenny did!"

"Mom, I want you to stay put. I'll be right over," Ray replied, really worried now about her emotional state.

"No, Raymond. I have some errands to run for Mrs. Cory. Besides, I think I'd like to be alone so I can think things out."

"Are you sure, Mom?" Ray asked, afraid to leave her by herself.

"I'm all right, Raymond. Honestly. I just needed to talk to someone, that's all. I've got to do the rest by myself," she said, summoning up her courage.

"If you need me, call me," he said reluctantly. "Okay? I'll be at the hotel all day, and if not, I'll leave word where you can reach me."

"Thank you. And Raymond, I'm sorry to be such a bother to you," Beatrice said apologetically.

"You couldn't be if you tried," he answered, meaning every word. "You're still my best girl!"

That evening, Ray called to check on his mother and was told by Rachel Cory that Beatrice had gone out for the evening with Jim Matthews. Ray breathed a sigh of relief. That was a good sign; it showed that his mother was not retreating into herself the way she had after Jenny left. Moreover, Beatrice had told him something of her friendship with Jim and as far as Ray was concerned, nothing could be better for his mother than to have a social life for once. It was probably the first time, too, he thought.

Taking advantage of his free time, Ray dialed Alice's number. "I'm sorry to be calling on such short notice, but I wanted to talk to you about Sally," he began, only partially telling the truth.

"Well, I haven't got plans for tonight, and Sally's at a friend's house for a slumber party. Would you like to come over?"

"I have a better idea," Ray said. "How about if I took you out to dinner? There's a new French restaurant that the hotel clerk was telling me about today."

Alice hesitated only for the briefest moment. She was sitting in her spacious living room, with its plush wall to wall carpeting, designer furniture, and painstakingly crafted stone fireplace and its panoramic bay windows . . . and she was alone. Even Sally had deserted her tonight. Getting out, seeing people might be just what she needed to boost her sagging spirits. Beyond that, Raymond had the uncanny ability, even under their somewhat awkward circumstances, to make her laugh.

"Dinner sounds like fun and I have been wanting to try L'Auberge—"

Ray didn't wait for her to finish the sentence. "I'll pick you up in twenty minutes."

"Wait, I'm not dressed for dinner."

"So dress fast," he said and hung up the phone.

Alice stared at the receiver for a moment. *He's certainly in a good mood,* she thought. Feeling suddenly giddy, almost like a high school girl getting ready for her first date, Alice sprinted up the stairs.

Ray Gordon was true to his word, arriving at Alice's house exactly twenty minutes after he'd hung up the phone.

The soft lights and intimate ambiance of L'Auberge may have been responsible for lulling Alice into a false sense of security as she gazed into Ray's warm and beckoning brown eyes across the small round table. The red wine also had something to do with it. For the first time in a long time, she felt truly relaxed. It was her first real evening out with a man since Steven died, she realized, and it felt good.

For his part, Ray successfully kept Alice laughing most of the evening with his stories. He couldn't seem to take his eyes off her. "You have a beautiful smile," he said at last, unable to simply gaze on her finely chiseled face without making some appropriate comment. Alice blushed like a school girl.

"Am I embarrassing you?" Ray asked, sensing her slight discomfort.

"Maybe, just a little," she replied, trying unsuccessfully to avert his gaze. "It's just that . . . well, Steven used to say that, too."

"Does that mean you still haven't been able to put his death behind you completely," Ray replied, feeling somewhat deflated.

"Steven and I loved each other for a very long time," Alice found herself explaining. "We had some rough times before we finally got married, but we got through them. Then, just when everything seemed perfect . . ." She looked away, barely able to continue. Ray wanted to pull her into his arms and make all the pain disappear, but it wouldn't have been right. For the moment, all he could do was respect Steve Frame's memory and do nothing.

"Sometimes, I can't believe he's never coming back," Alice went on at last, her voice filled with emotion. "That's why I can't bear the thought of losing Sally, too. I've lost so much in my life, Raymond. I don't think I could take any more." Try as she might to control herself, Alice realized that her face was wet with tears. Ray moved his chair over next to hers and slipped his arm around her protectively.

"I won't let you lose Sally," he whispered. "I promise you."

Alice looked at him, her lashes wet with tears. "But, what about your mother? I don't understand."

Neither did Ray himself, not completely. All he knew was that he would not let Alice down. Somehow, someway, he would convince Beatrice to drop her suit.

It wasn't that Ray didn't care about his mother's feelings. He did, a great deal. But he also sensed that Beatrice was beginning to back down all by herself. Once the urgency of the situation had dissipated, he was sure his mother would see things more realistically. Ray was also convinced that Alice would never deprive Beatrice of the right to see the child and be a real grandmother to her.

"I know this isn't going to be easy for you, Alice," he said later, as they sat over after-dinner coffees back in her living room, "but you've got to be patient for just a little while longer. My mother knows in her heart that Sally should stay with you. She just hasn't admitted it yet."

Alice felt enormously relieved all of a sudden. "Do you really think so?"

"Absolutely. You've got to understand what a shock all of this has been to her. She's just starting to wind down from it now. I'm going to keep talking to her, so don't you worry."

Alice looked at him for a long time in silence. There was a wonderful gentleness about him. He was strong and forceful, yet also compassionate and tender. For a moment, she almost wished she could lean her head against his inviting shoulder and be held like Steven used to hold her. But she stopped herself.

"Why are you doing this?" Alice asked, suddenly curious.

Ray gazed into her wide blue eyes, and right then he knew for certain that she was the most special woman he'd met in years. Instinctively, he reached out and touched Alice's face. "I don't want anyone to ever hurt you, ever again," he whispered softly. Alice felt herself melting under the warmth of his touch.

"Oh, Raymond . . ." she sighed. She didn't know how or why, but she felt him gently, softly kiss her, and she was completely and totally intoxicated.

"Alice," he whispered, continuing to kiss her, letting some of the passion he had been locking away finally escape. To her surprise, she was responding, drinking in his kisses like someone dying of thirst, until she finally caught herself and pulled away. They both looked away, their faces red with shock and embarrassment and exhilaration.

"I'm sorry. I shouldn't have done that," he said, rather awkwardly as he quickly got up off the sofa and reached for his coat.

Alice followed him to the door. "It's all right," she said, aware that her cheeks were still flushed. "It just happened. I know it didn't mean anything."

Ray looked at her for a long moment. He reached out and gently stroked a strand of her hair, which glistened in the soft, evening light. "I wish that were true. But it's not . . . at least not for me." He turned quickly and walked back to his rented car, started the ignition and backed out of her driveway without looking back once.

Alice watched him drive away, his car kicking up crystalline flurries of silver-white snow as it disappeared down the drive. She touched her lips reflexively. "It's not true for me, either," she whispered.

Chapter Eight
A Seduction Fails

Rachel was immensely pleased with herself when she woke up in her husband's arms the next morning. After seeing him in Tall Boys with his lovely lunch partner and then getting Iris's call to add fuel to the fire, Rachel was afraid Mac might be turning away from her. But after last night, she felt perfectly secure. Mac had made love to her with the tenderness and passion of a man hopelessly in love, and she had responded eagerly, allowing herself to become utterly immersed in the depth and fire of his emotion. Let Iris try to ruin that, Rachel thought, smiling as Mac began to stir.

He opened his eyes and kissed her. "Good morning, darling," he said softly.

Rachel snuggled into the security of his embrace. "Did you sleep well?"

"Like a baby!" He kissed her again. "How did I get so lucky to find such a wonderful and exciting wife?"

"I'm the lucky one," she replied, meaning it with all her heart.

"We're both lucky, and let's not ever forget it," he said, getting out of bed.

"Can't you stay in bed a while longer?"

"If I do, I'll never get to the office" he replied with a laugh. "But you rest, darling. I'll have Beatrice bring you up a breakfast tray." Mac went into the bathroom and ran his shower.

Rachel stretched like a contented cat. Yes, she thought, it was very nice to be Mrs. Mac Cory and to be loved by the best and most wonderful man in the world. She had been lucky indeed.

At his office, Mac was about to leave for an editorial meeting when Iris whirled in, all bundled up in a silver-gray, full-length fox coat. "I'm so glad I caught you, Daddy," she said breathlessly.

"I'm just on my way to a meeting," he protested, trying to get past her. "I don't have time to talk."

"But this will only take a minute," she assured him.

Mac frowned, aware that he had very little choice but to hear his daughter out.

"Oh, by the way, I hope Rachel didn't get the wrong idea when I told her about you and Tracey having lunch," she mentioned as they went back into Mac's office. She hoped to get the lowdown on what had transpired in the Cory house last night.

"Why would you talk to Rachel about that?" Mac questioned.

"Didn't she tell you I called?" Iris asked, genuinely surprised and totally disappointed.

"No. And besides, I told her I had lunch with Tracey myself. Now what is this all about, Iris?"

Damn that Rachel, anyway! Iris thought. Obviously the little witch had outfoxed her this time, but it was only a temporary victory, of that Iris was certain.

"I don't know what you mean, Daddy," Iris replied, her eyes wide with feigned innocence.

"You're trying to cause trouble between Rachel and me and I won't have it," Mac stated firmly.

"Daddy, please, I just came over to ask you to stop by my house for drinks on your way home."

"Forget it!" Mac snapped. "Now if you'll excuse me, I have a room full of employees waiting."

Iris changed her tactics immediately. "But, Daddy, Tracey will be terribly upset if you don't come!"

"What's Tracey got to do with it?" he asked impatiently.

"Well, you see, I told her that you wanted to stop by tonight and look through the photographs she took in Napal. She's so insecure about doing that photo journal as it is. If you don't come, you'll destroy her confidence once and for all." Iris watched her father closely, waiting for his reaction.

Mac sighed heavily. "You should never have told her that I would come over without checking with me first. Rachel and I might have had plans for this evening."

"Well do you?" she asked, her lovely face puckered almost into a frown.

"No, but—"

Iris didn't let him get another word out, but instead threw her arms around his neck and kissed him sweetly on the cheek. "Oh, Daddy, I knew you wouldn't disappoint me."

"I haven't said yes yet. I'll have to call Rachel and be sure she won't be alone in the house."

"But it'll only be for an hour. Surely Rachel can do without you for that long," she quipped, her disapproval beginning to surface.

Mac wasn't about to be pushed into a corner. "I told you, I'll check with Rachel and then I'll let you know." He stepped swiftly around her and headed down the long corridor.

Iris gritted her teeth. There was no way Rachel was going

to interfere with what she had planned for tonight. In fact, she was going to make doubly sure of that by calling Rachel herself. Tonight belonged to Iris, and with Tracey's help, Mac just might walk out of her house a new and hopefully freer man.

That afternoon, Rachel was surprised when Mac came home for lunch with a dozen long-stemmed roses.

"What's the occasion?" Rachel asked, kissing him with delight.

"Does there have to be one?" Mac asked.

"I guess not. You're certainly in a good mood," she observed. "Why don't you play hookey for the rest of the day and stay with me?" she asked.

"I wish I could, darling, but I've got meetings all afternoon."

"Well, then, we'll just have to make lunch extra special. How about if we have a tray sent upstairs?"

Mac smiled wickedly. "You must have read my mind."

After they'd made love, Rachel felt about as happy and secure as she could remember ever feeling. Thus, when Mac mentioned Iris's visit to the complex, she wasn't even slightly troubled.

"Iris asked me to stop over tonight for drinks so I could look at Tracey's photographs, but I told her I had to check with you first."

Rachel mulled it over for a moment. That woman never gave up. She was determined to come between Rachel and Mac, and Rachel was equally determined to beat her at her own game.

"I don't mind if you stop off at Iris's after work, Mac," Rachel answered finally. She knew, of course, that Iris had something or other up her sleeve. But for the first time, she was taking her mother's advice and playing it very cool. If she acted like a silly, jealous housewife, as Iris fully expected her to do, she might as well hand Mac over to Tracey DeWitt on a silver platter. Let Iris think she had the upper hand, Rachel thought. She'd see soon enough that she didn't.

Later, Iris called Rachel to test the waters herself.

"Daddy said he was stopping by after work," she began. "Of course, if it really bothers you dear, especially since Tracey will be there, I'll understand."

Rachel smiled. Was she ever going to give Iris a run for her money this time. "Why should it bother me?" Rachel asked nonchalantly.

"Well, as you know, Daddy and Tracey were quite close at one time."

"Water under the dam, Iris," Rachel said breezily, aware that she had to be boiling mad.

Iris arched her brow. "Of course you're welcome to come, too, but in your condition—"

Rachel cut her off. "I'm afraid I have a sculpting lesson this afternoon anyway. But thank you so much for thinking of me." Rachel hung up the phone and couldn't help laughing out loud. It was the best she'd felt in a long, long time.

Iris, however, couldn't say the same. For some reason, Rachel had changed. Iris detected a very different tone in her voice. What had happened, she wondered, to effect such a metamorphosis? Whatever it was, Iris was quite sure it was only temporary. Or could it possibly have anything to do with Ken Palmer, her sculpting instructor? she wondered. Ever since the attractive, irreverent young man had started coming to the house to give Rachel private instructions, Iris had noticed that Rachel had been arranging it so that Mac would be out during their lessons. It made Iris angrier than anything to see her father being made such a fool of right under his nose. Well, she consoled herself, if things went as she planned, Tracey might just be able to change all that. Then Rachel would be right back where she belonged—behind the eight ball.

Later that afternoon, Ada went over to the Cory house to bring her daughter some homemade chicken soup. Although she wasn't an alarmist, Ada had a queer feeling about Rachel's pregnancy. For one thing, she wasn't following Dave Gilchrist's orders to take it easy. Rachel wasn't the kind of woman to ever sit still for too long. Ada had hoped that since Mac built her the sculpture studio in the house, she would be more inclined to stay home and work with her clay models and just concentrate all her energies on having a healthy baby. Nothing doing. Rachel wasn't happy unless she was involved in something, and now it seemed to be Beatrice's problems.

"I hope you took my advice about Beatrice," Ada said fixing her daughter with a warning look.

"If you came here to lecture me again, Mom, you can just turn right around and leave," Rachel cautioned, not at all tolerant of her mother's badgering.

"I said my piece. I promise, I won't mention it again."

"Thank you."

"Now eat your soup," Ada ordered, setting a bowl and spoon out for her daughter.

"I had lunch already, with Mac."

"So you'll have some more," Ada quipped. "What are you afraid of, gaining weight?"

Rachel shook her head. "You're a real comedian, you know that."

"That's what they tell me."

"Well, since Mac probably won't be home for a while, I guess a little soup wouldn't hurt."

"Mac working late again?" Ada asked.

Rachel raised an eyebrow. "In a way. He went over to Iris's for cocktails."

Ada did a double-take. "You mean you let Mac go over to Iris's house and you're not even mad?"

Rachel shrugged. "Why should I be?"

"Because you're always mad when he spends any time with her, especially alone."

True enough, Rachel thought. And certainly with good enough reason. She knew Iris took every opportunity to poison Mac's mind against her and normally that would make her feel very insecure. But not tonight. Not anymore. She was beginning to realize that the only way to fight Iris was to ignore her completely. Of course, after the beautiful night she and Mac had spent together, it was easy to feel cocky where Iris was concerned. For now, anyway. She wasn't sure about tomorrow. But she did have one ace up her sleeve: what she had overheard Iris tell Tracey about her marriage to Robert. Mac would certainly not be pleased when he found out. And it only served Iris right that Rachel should tell him. After all, Iris had arranged this whole evening of seduction with Tracy to ruin her father's marriage. Why shouldn't Rachel get her licks in, too? But even more than all of that, Rachel thought, poor Clarice deserved a better shake, and telling Mac might just kill two birds with one stone.

"Iris is trying to set Mac up with Tracey DeWitt," she admitted to her mother.

Ada stared back in shock. "And you just let him go over there?"

"I trust Mac."

"Well I should hope so. But it's Iris I'm worried about," Ada remarked.

"I have a little surprise in store for her, so don't you worry," Rachel said, chuckling.

"Whatever you're thinking, forget it!" Ada warned. "That woman's got a trick up both sleeves and then some. Just stay away from her, do you hear me, Rachel?"

"Would you stop worrying," she told her mother, trying to laugh it all off. Rachel knew full well what she was doing, and Iris was going to regret the day she'd ever tried to ruin her marriage to Mac, that much Rachel promised herself.

Tracey was dressed to kill when she opened the front door to let Mac inside. For a moment, he just stared at her. Tall and stately, she looked like a vision out of a high fashion magazine. Her long, lustrous hair was pulled back off her face and knotted into a chignon at the nape of her swan-like neck. She was wearing a form-fitting, deep purple sequined dress that fell fashionably just below her knee, showing off her shapely legs in their smoke-gray, silk stockings to perfection.

"You're right on time," she said, linking her arm through his and leading him into the drawing room. "I really appreciate your taking the time to look at my photographs."

"You happen to be an excellent photographer and if it's encouragement you need to get that book of yours together, that's exactly what I'm going to give you," Mac replied, smiling at her perfectly oval face, with it's finely chiseled cheekbones.

"Well, I'm going to need a whole lot of that," Tracey confided, squeezing his arm just enough to let him know she was interested.

Mac smiled somewhat uncomfortably as Iris whirled into the room and went straight over to her father, giving him a big hug.

"I'm so glad you decided to come, Daddy!"

"You can thank Rachel. She's the one who didn't plan anything for us this evening."

Iris smiled. "Oh, yes, that art instructor of hers is coming over, isn't he?"

Mac tugged at his tie, looking uncomfortable. To be

honest, he didn't like the idea of Ken Palmer coming over to the house to give Rachel those private lessons. For one thing, he put too many ideas into Rachel's head. The sculpting was only supposed to be a hobby for her, but now, because of Ken's influence and encouragement, it was becoming a good deal more. Rachel was even talking about giving her own art exhibition sometime in the future. Well, Mac reasoned, she'd get that foolishness out of her head as soon as the baby was born. Then she'd be far too busy to think of being a professional artist. Not that Mac really minded Rachel having a career of her own, he just didn't want her to overdo it.

"Rachel enjoys her sculpting lessons, Iris. They're a good outlet for her."

"Oh, I agree," Tracey offered enthusiastically. "That's what my photography is for me."

"Oh, but darling, you're a professional," Iris noted, making it plain that she thought Rachel was certainly nothing of the sort.

"How is your wife?" Tracey asked. "I'd love us all to get together some time."

"I'm sure you two would get on famously," Mac replied. "I'm sure Rachel would love to talk with you about art. And she'd love to be able to pal out with someone as stylish as you are."

"Why, thank you. What a lovely compliment!"

Iris exchanged a look with her friend. *So Daddy has noticed,* she thought. *Soon he'll see how much more suited Tracey is to him than that—that tacky little wife of his!*

Throughout the cocktail hour, Mac kept glancing at his watch, which irritated Iris to no end. Robert finally sauntered in an hour late and immediately he and Mac retreated to the study. Now Iris was really fit to be tied, and she lit into Tracey.

"Why didn't you say something?" she hissed.

"What did you expect me to do, drag Mac back into the room? He's obviously not interested."

"That's absurd, darling. And even if it were true, you of all people should know how to get him interested. Daddy's crazy about you!"

"I think that's all in the past now," Tracey remarked, trying to camouflage her disappointment.

"You can't give up on me," Iris exclaimed, thoroughly frustrated. "You're the only one who can help Daddy see what he's missing."

"Maybe he doesn't want to, Iris," Tracey offered. "Maybe he's quite happy with Rachel."

"Nonsense," Iris snapped, waving her perfectly manicured fingers as if to dispel the very notion. "Daddy just doesn't know his own mind. Rachel has him so completely wrapped around her little finger it's disgusting!"

Tracey merely knitted her finely penciled brows together skeptically. Just then, the phone began to ring. Iris snatched up the receiver, in no mood to exchange pleasantries with anyone.

"Yes, what is it?" she answered abruptly.

"Iris, it's Rachel," the rather strange-sounding voice on the other end said.

"What do you want, Rachel?" Iris snapped, shooting Tracey an exasperated look.

Rachel's voice was weak and Iris could barely hear her. "Please get Mac. I've got to speak to him."

"Daddy and Robert are locked up in the study discussing important business. I have no intention of disturbing them." With that, she slammed the phone down. "Now do you see what I mean about Rachel?" Iris asked her friend. "The little witch can't leave Daddy alone for a moment. She's always at him!"

Thirty seconds later, the phone rang again. "Hello," Iris bellowed.

123

"Please, Iris, please put Mac on," came Rachel's whispery voice.

"What is wrong with you? I told you Daddy is busy!"

"Iris, this is important. I don't feel well. Please, I've got to talk to Mac!" Iris could tell she was crying. "Iris, I'm begging you . . ." Rachel sobbed.

"Why don't you grow up? When Daddy is finished, I'll tell him you called." Again she slammed the phone down.

"That was Rachel again?" Tracey asked.

"Yes, can you believe her gall?"

"Maybe it's important, Iris."

"What could Rachel have to say that could ever be important?" Iris laughed, pouring them each another glass of champagne.

In the study, Mac noticed Robert's low spirits.

"Is there anything wrong between you and Iris?" he asked, the concern apparent in his voice.

Robert rested his chin on his hands and looked down at the carpet for several moments.

"We're having some problems," he admitted finally. "But I think we can work them out."

"I know my daughter can be very exasperating sometimes, Robert, but you've got to show her who's boss," Mac told him. Elliot Carrington, Iris's first husband, had made the mistake of giving in to his wife's every whim until he'd just had enough and that was the end of the marriage. Mac didn't want to see that happen to Iris again, but inwardly he had strong misgivings about whether Robert, with his soft-spoken, gentlemanly manner, was the man to tame his daughter. In fact, Iris's whole hasty marriage troubled him no end, particularly since it was common knowledge that Robert and Clarice had been seeing one another at the time.

"I'm thinking of taking a job in Washington," Robert

told his father-in-law. "Maybe Iris and I wouldn't fight so much if we started fresh, away from Bay City."

"Well, naturally I'd hate to see you go," Mac began, "but if it's what you and Iris want . . ."

"Iris doesn't know about it, really," Robert admitted. "The last time I even broached the subject was after my trip to D.C., and she wouldn't even discuss it."

Mac frowned. That sounded like Iris all right. And if Robert thought he was going to take her away from Bay City, he was a fool indeed. That left only one alternative as Mac saw it and he wasn't one bit happy about it. Then he had an idea. "Maybe the two of you should take a trip. Why not take a cruise down to the Caribbean or something? This is the perfect time of year for it. I'll even make all the arrangements myself, if you like," Mac said, hoping to encourage his son-in-law.

"I've got too much work, Mac. I can't even think about taking time off until spring."

"That could be part of the problem," Mac commented, wanting to help.

"I know. Iris thinks I'm supposed to be with her twenty-four hours a day," Robert sighed in exasperation.

"I'm sure the two of you can find some middle ground."

Robert got up from his leather chair and went over to the window. He peered out onto the long, snow-covered lawn. Suddenly he found himself thinking of Clarice. What was she doing now? he wondered. A powerful urge took hold of him. He didn't know why, but he had to see her.

"I'm sure everything will work out between you and Iris," Mac said, wishfully.

Robert turned around. He smiled sadly. "I'm sure, too."

When the men finally came out of the study, Iris had coffee waiting.

"I really must be getting home," Mac protested as his daughter led him over to the sofa right next to Tracey.

"Don't be silly, you have time for coffee!" Tracey shot Iris a troubled look. Afraid her friend was going to mention Rachel's call, Iris flashed her a warning glare. Reluctantly, Tracey sat back and sipped her coffee.

"I'll have to call Rachel and tell her I'll be late," Mac said, getting up and heading for the phone. Iris was trapped. Did she dare admit to her father that Rachel had already called, or should she wait for Rachel to tell him? It was a no-win situation. Whatever she did, her father was sure to be angry so Iris decided to grit her teeth and leave the ball in Rachel's court.

A few minutes later, Mac came back into the parlor.

"The line was busy. Rachel must be talking to Ada."

Iris breathed a sigh of relief. The fates were indeed with her, she thought. "Maybe she just took it off the hook," Iris replied innocently.

"Why would she do that?" Mac asked, puzzled.

"Well, she is working with that sculpting instructor of hers . . . maybe she just didn't want to be disturbed." Iris could see her father's expression darken. Obviously, Rachel's shaggy-haired tutor was not a popular subject.

Tracey figured out Iris's game immediately, and decided to turn the tables on her. "How is Rachel progressing with her work?" she asked. Iris fixed her friend with an irritated glare.

"She's a very talented young woman," Mac said, beaming with pride. "I just hope Rachel's art doesn't get so important to her that I have to compete with it for her attention!"

Tracey smiled. "You must love her very much."

"I guess it shows, huh?" Mac replied. Tracey felt her own spirits plummet. Iris couldn't have been more wrong. Mac was definitely in love with his wife, and from all indications, Rachel felt the same way about him. Whatever Tracey and Mac had shared had been left somewhere on the streets of Paris, many years ago. There was no resurrecting it, and for that Tracey was profoundly sorry. But she was also a realist. If Mac was still in love with his wife, then fine. Tracey would find another man, and perhaps right here in Bay City.

For her part, Iris was appalled by her friend's behavior. After all the trouble she had taken to put Tracey and Mac together, Tracey had just spoiled the whole thing. Iris narrowed her eyes with determination. There was no way she would let her friend back out of their bargain.

Beatrice was pretty disturbed when she met Ada at the diner that evening. The strain of the whole business about Sally was getting to her. More and more, she had come to realize that she couldn't bear to hurt Alice by taking her child away from her. On the other hand, she didn't want to disappoint Rachel either. Her employer had been so supportive and generous; how could she turn around and tell her that it had all been for naught?

"You don't have to worry about Rachel's feelings," Ada assured her friend. "I know she thought she was doing the right thing by encouraging you, but I think we both know what's really right."

Beatrice exhaled deeply. "I wasn't a very good mother, was I?"

"We all make mistakes, Bea."

"Ada, I didn't even know my own daughter was pregnant. She ran away and never told me. What does that say about my suitability to raise Sally?"

Ada put her hand comfortingly over her friend's. "Look, that's all in the past. The point is, you're beyond the child-rearing stage, Bea. You should be enjoying life now. Like I said, let Alice do the mothering. You just be a doting grandmother."

Beatrice took her friend's words to heart. Perhaps it was

time she started to live her own life. Sally would certainly be happier with Alice, and they could all go on just as they had, only now Sally would know she had a grandmother. That wasn't so bad, was it? she asked herself.

Alice was lying on the sofa with an ice pack on her head. Several times already, she had been tempted to reach for the phone and call Raymond. What had happened the night before couldn't just be ignored. Then again, what could she do about it? After all, it was only a little kiss. What harm was there in that? As she tossed and turned, the front doorbell rang. She sat up and put the ice bag on the coffee table. Alice wasn't expecting anyone, but she sure could use some company right about now, she thought. If nothing else, it might take her mind off her problems.

She walked gingerly to the door and opened to find Ray Gordon standing there. Alice didn't know why, but she felt her heart skip a beat.

"Ray . . ." Suddenly, she didn't know what else to say.

"Hello, Alice," he said, a bit awkwardly. "I was hoping we could talk." Alice showed him into the living room. She could see he was troubled and for a moment, she thought there was some new development about Sally.

"Has Beatrice said anything to you?" she asked, instantly concerned.

"I didn't come here about Sally. I came because of last night. . . ." His voice trailed off and Alice could feel her cheeks getting hot. She could tell Raymond felt the same way she did.

"You don't have to say anything," Alice replied, a bit embarrassed.

"I had no right to come on to you like that," he apologized, looking down at the floor.

"We were both lonely. That's all there was to it," she stressed, trying to convince herself as well as Raymond.

"Then, you're not angry with me?"

"Of course not. You've been a good friend, Raymond. Your kindness these last few weeks has meant a lot to me."

Ray looked into Alice's clear, compassionate eyes. If it were up to him, he would be there to support her for the rest of his life. "I've come to care about you and Sally a great deal," he admitted, not even fully aware himself of just how much.

Alice reached out and touched his arm. "Your wife is a very lucky woman," she said softly.

The thought of Olive was like a jolt to Ray Gordon's system. How different the two women were: Alice was so gentle and giving; Olive so harsh and demanding. From the moment she'd answered the front door and invited him in the day of Sally's birthday party, Alice had been the focus of Ray's dreams. But now he knew that had to stop. Alice was still in love with Steve Frame, even if he could never come back to her. And Ray was himself a married man with two sons. Until and unless those things changed, he had no right to fall in love with Alice.

"I guess you'll be going back to California soon?" Alice commented, trying to lighten the tension between them.

"I'll wait until everything's been squared away with you and my mother," Ray said. "I'm going to talk to her again tomorrow and see if we can't resolve this."

"Thank you. I really appreciate all you've done." Alice said softly.

"If ever you need anything, anything at all, I want you to know that you can always call on me," Ray offered.

She smiled in appreciation. "I know, Raymond."

After that, Ray got his coat and went back to his hotel. No sooner had Ray turned the key in the door than the phone began to ring.

"Are you ever coming home, Ray, or have you decided to camp out in Bay City forever?" Olive Gordon asked shrilly when he answered the phone.

"I still have a few more things to straighten up here," he replied, somewhat taken aback by her tone.

"You're still not planning to bring that kid back with you, are you?"

"No, Sally will be staying here in Bay City."

"Well if it's not the kid, who is keeping you there?"

"Just a few loose ends," Ray assured her. But as he hung up, he couldn't keep Alice Frame's face from appearing in his mind.

Chapter Nine
The Dam Bursts

Robert walked into the diner, grateful to be away from the drawing room pretentiousness of his own home; rather, of his wife's home, for he had never really felt as if he belonged there. Every room, every piece of furniture down to the towels in the bathrooms, bore Iris's signature. He let out a long sigh of relief. It was nice to be in a place where he felt comfortable for a change. As he sat on a stool at the counter, Clarice whirled out of the kitchen carrying an order in each hand. She stopped short for a moment as her eyes met Robert's. If she could have, she would have bolted for the door. Instead, she hurried out onto the floor and served the dinners.

A few minutes later, she was back behind the counter.

"Can I get you something?" she asked Robert, mentally counting down the minutes before her shift ended.

"Just coffee," he replied, looking at her steadily.

Clarice turned to get the pot. Her hand instinctively shot up to her face. As she suspected, her cheeks were burning. She only hoped Robert hadn't noticed the effect he still had on her. "Are you sure you don't want something to go with that?" she asked, turning around, her eye on the clock.

"How's Cory?" Robert asked, cutting through the small talk.

"He's just fine," Clarice replied. She bit at her lower lip.

"Is something wrong, Clarice?" he asked, knowing full well she was always uncomfortable in his presence lately.

Finally the last minute ticked away. "My shift's over. I've got to get home."

As she started out of the diner, he grabbed her wrist. "Let me drive you." The tone of his voice was soft and gentle, just as Clarice remembered it had been when they were lovers. But she couldn't allow herself to give in to her feelings. Robert was beyond her reach now. Iris had seen to that. All Clarice wanted was to be left in peace with her little boy.

"Thanks, but the bus passes by right outside."

"Please, Clarice. I'd just like to drive you home. Maybe I could even stop in and see Cory?"

Clarice could feel herself softening. Robert hadn't been up to her place since they'd split up. But there was no way she was going to set herself up for another fall. "Please let go. I'll miss my bus."

Robert looked into her wide blue eyes. "Clarice . . ."

She pulled her wrist away from him and grabbed her coat. "Good-bye, Robert."

He watched as her slim figure hurried out into the dark street. Suddenly he felt cold and completely alone.

Iris was trying to cajole her father into staying for dinner, and she wasn't having much success at it. To her increasing displeasure, Tracey wasn't lifting one finger to help, either.

"I'm sure Rachel won't mind if you have dinner with us," she protested.

"I'm sorry, Iris, but I promised Rachel I'd be back. I should have left an hour ago."

"Obviously Rachel is still busy with her sculpting lesson," she said, hoping to incense her father into agreeing. But he wasn't taking the bait.

"We'll do it some other time," Mac said, getting up from the sofa.

Tracey got up, too. "I hope we'll all get together again before I leave," she said sincerely.

"Well, of course we'll get together." Iris's voice was shrill as she gave her friend a look that could kill.

As Mac headed for the door, Iris's maid, Louise, came in looking terribly upset.

"Mr. Cory, there's a call for you."

Iris squared her jaw. *Damn that Rachel,* she thought. *She just won't rest until she steals Daddy away from us!*

"Who is it, Louise?" Mac asked.

"A Mr. Palmer. He said it's about Mrs. Cory."

Mac's face immediately registered concern as he hurried out with Louise to the phone. Tracey looked at Iris.

"You should have told him about Rachel's call. I told you it might have been important."

Iris dismissed it completely. "He's probably calling to see if Daddy's left yet, that's all."

"Really, Iris, that is so absurd!"

Mac came running back into the room, his face white with fear.

"I've got to get back right away."

"What is it, Daddy?"

"Ken Palmer says he's been ringing the bell at the house and no one is answering."

"Rachel's probably taking a nap," Iris said, unbothered.

"She was all alone over there. I don't know what's happened, but I don't like it."

As he raced toward the door, Iris called after him. "Call me, Daddy . . . just so I know everything's all right."

Tracey shook her head. "I hope you haven't done something you're really going to regret."

Mac got back home with unprecedented speed. He raced into the living room. "Rachel? Where are you, darling?" Suddenly he stopped short. "Oh, my God!"

Behind his massive desk, Rachel lay slumped on the floor, the phone receiver dangling limply beside her. Mac put his hand gently to his wife's face.

"Rachel? Can you hear me, darling?" She didn't answer. Her face felt so hot, Mac thought, seized with panic. Shaking himself out of it, he reconnected the phone and then called for an ambulance. Carrying his unconscious wife to the sofa, he covered her with a blanket. She looked so pale and small under the thick, mohair throw, almost like a little child who'd fallen asleep. Mac took her limp hand in his.

"Please don't leave me, Rachel. I love you so much!"

Soon the paramedics arrived and were lifting Rachel onto a stretcher.

"She's pregnant," Mac informed them. Then he thought, *Good Lord, what if something happens to the baby?* But Mac drove the thought out of his mind. The important thing now was to get Rachel to the hospital, and time was of the essence.

He dialed Ada's number, but there was no answer. Then he called Iris and Robert answered.

Mac's voice was hoarse and urgent. "Rachel is sick. She's being rushed to Bay General. Please keep calling Ada until you get her, and tell her to come right away."

"Of course. Is there anything else I can do?" he asked, concerned.

"Pray." The line went dead. Robert stood by the phone for a moment, stunned.

"Who was that darling?" Iris asked sweetly as she and Tracey entered the foyer.

134

"Mac . . ."

"Oh, yes. I told Daddy to let us know that everything was all right."

"It isn't." Robert turned and faced his wife. "It's Rachel. They've just taken her to the hospital."

Tracey's hand shot up to her mouth to suppress a gasp. Her eyes met Iris's.

Now what kind of a game was Rachel playing? Iris wondered.

"I told you to tell Mac when Rachel called," Tracey said, pulling her friend aside and feeling equally guilty.

Iris whirled on her sharply. "How was I to know she was ill? Rachel should have said something."

"You didn't give her much of a chance, Iris."

Suddenly, Iris felt a wave of panic overtake her. "Tracey, you mustn't let anyone know that Rachel called. Especially Daddy."

"What if something dreadful happens?" Tracey asked, not wanting any part of her friend's deception.

"Don't be silly. Pregnant women are always fainting or something. I'm sure Rachel will be back home tomorrow."

"In that case, she'll probably tell Mac all about the phone call."

Yes, Iris thought, *Rachel would do just that.* If Mac ever found out, he would certainly be furious with her. And then Rachel would have exactly what she wanted: Mac Cory all to herself. Perhaps she had been underestimating Rachel, Iris considered. But first things first. She had to make sure Rachel never breathed a word of those calls to Mac. Otherwise there would definitely be hell to pay, and Iris would be the one paying it!

At Bay City General Hospital, Mac paced anxiously outside the emergency room door. It was all his fault, he told himself. He should have never left Rachel alone for so long. He looked up, his face drawn and weary, and saw Ada coming through the revolving doors. He waved her over.

"What happened?" she asked, almost afraid to hear what Mac was going to say. "She didn't lose the baby, did she?"

"They're examining her now." He pounded his fists against the wall. "This should never have happened. I should have been there."

Ada remembered Rachel telling her earlier that Mac was stopping over to Iris's after work. She remembered, too, having a strange feeling about that although it wasn't really anything she could have put into words at the time. "There's no way you could have known, Mac" she reassured him.

"If anything happens to Rachel, Ada . . ." his voice trailed off.

"Rachel's a strong girl. She's going to be fine."

Just then, Dave Gilchrist came out of the emergency room. His face was tense and agitated.

"What is it, Dave," Mac asked, his tone guarded.

"We're going to have to keep Rachel here over night and do some tests, Mac."

"What do you suspect is wrong?"

"She's not going to lose the baby, is she?" Ada asked.

"It's too soon to tell, Ada," Dave replied cautiously, turning toward Rachel's mother. Looking back at Mac, he added, "Why don't we go and fill out the admission forms?"

"Can't I see her?" he asked.

"She'll be in her room in a few minutes."

Ada linked her arm with Mac's. "C'mon, we'll see Rachel in a few minutes."

By the time John Randolph arrived home from the office, he felt absolutely numb. In fact, he had driven aimlessly around town for an hour or so, trying to make sense of what Barbara told him about Marianne. He still couldn't believe it. His own daughter was unable to confide in him about a decision that would affect her whole life. What was happening to his family, he wondered. Had things changed so drastically without his even knowing it? It seemed as though only months ago they were a happy family: laughing together, planning things, having summer picnics. Now it was all over. The winter had descended and with it, a kind of deathly quiet secrecy had locked them all into a tomb-like silence. Marianne, his beloved daughter, had betrayed him, and why? He could not fathom it. And even worse, the rest of the family had known all about it and had elected not to tell him. *But why*, John asked himself, *why?*

Pat came into the living room with the evening paper and stopped short when she saw her husband standing in the middle of the room, staring at the floor. "John? Are you all right?" she asked.

He looked up at her, his eyes vacant and unfocused.

"John, please, tell me. You're frightening me," Pat said, aware now that something was terribly wrong.

John started over toward her, shaking his head. Pat felt herself backing up with a feeling of dread.

"You knew, didn't you?" he asked in an accusing tone.

A flood of panic engulfed Pat. She knew that sooner or later it was going to come to this. She'd warned Marianne again and again, she begged her to tell her father the truth. Now it was too late. John had found out in the worst possible way. Now it would look as though his whole family had been conspiring against him.

"You knew Marianne went to New York to get an abortion, didn't you?"

"No . . . not right away," Pat replied, her voice shaking.

"Were any of you ever going to tell me?" he spat out.

"I begged Marianne to talk to you, John. She was just so ashamed . . . I'm so sorry."

ANOTHER WORLD

"Sorry? My daughter gets pregnant and doesn't tell me, then she has an abortion and everyone knows about it but her own father. Do you really think that 'sorry' covers all that?"

"You're right. It doesn't," Pat replied with both shame and embarrassment. She suddenly felt she had handled the whole situation very badly. She should have taken Dave Gilchrist's advice and been more firm with Marianne. Pat should not have let herself be put in so untenable a position. Of course, none of that mattered anymore. The damage, extensive as it was, had already been done.

"I had to find out from Aunt Liz," John railed. "Do you have any idea how that made me feel?"

Pat thought she must be hearing things. "Aunt Liz? That's impossible. How could she have known anything?"

"Apparently she heard Marianne talking to Barbara about it."

Pat could not believe her ears. Aunt Liz had a habit of interfering in all their lives, but even she couldn't be this calloused and indifferent to their feelings. Or could she?

"Even if Marianne couldn't bring herself to tell me, Pat, why couldn't you?"

"I gave her my word, John," Pat repeated, knowing how lame her words sounded. And as soon as she said them, she realized how insipid they were. John was her husband. No matter what Marianne said, Pat had no right to promise not to tell him anything. It was wrong. It was against everything she believed a family should be. If Marianne had been too immature to consider that, Pat certainly should have insisted that her daughter do the right thing. And if Marianne would not, it was Pat's duty to speak to John about it. But all she had done was sit back and wring her hands, waiting for the dam to burst. Now it had, and she felt herself drowning in her own bad judgment.

"John, I never meant to hurt you . . ." she began. But her husband wasn't really listening to her anymore. He had

138

been cut to the quick and she knew in her heart that he blamed her.

"You know, Pat, you've always treated me like a stranger in my own house. Since the day we were married, something has always been missing. You've always held something back."

"That's not true—" she tried to protest.

But John was relentless. "The only reason you married me was because I got you cleared of Tom Baxter's murder."

Pat was shocked. She felt as though she had been hit in the face with a ton of bricks. "How can you say that? After all the years we've been married. How?"

John looked her squarely in the eyes. "You've never been completely open with me. This is just the last straw," he bellowed, turning around and heading for the door.

"Where are you going?"

"Away. I'm not staying in a house where I'm treated like an outsider."

Not knowing what else to do, Pat grabbed her husband's arm. "If you'd only let me explain it from the beginning," she pleaded.

"I think it's a little late for that, don't you, Pat?" He wrenched his arm free and grabbed his coat from the hall closet.

"Please, John, don't do this," Pat begged, as tears began to well in her eyes. "What'll I tell Michael and Marianne?"

John studied his wife a moment. "Does it really matter?" Before she could get another word out, the door slammed with a thud. A moment later, Pat heard the engine of John's car start up, and then the skidding sound of tires as it sped out of the driveway. She put both her hands to her temples. Her head was throbbing like never before. Instinctively, she reached for the phone and began to dial a number.

"This is Mrs. Randolph. Would you page Dr. Gilchrist. It's urgent!"

"I'm sorry, ma'am, but the doctor has an emergency right now. Can he call you back?"

Pat felt her head spinning. She had to talk to Dave or she didn't know what she might do. "Just ask him to call me back as soon as possible, please." She hung up the phone and looked around the room. The Christmas tree was still up, and there was a fire in the fireplace. Everything looked the same, but nothing was. It had all suddenly exploded. And it was all her fault and Liz Matthews's.

When Pat rang her doorbell unexpectedly a half an hour later, Aunt Liz seemed unbelievably pleased. So rarely did any of the family seek her out. It was always she who had to do the seeking.

"Pat, what a surprise. Come in. I was just about to make some tea."

"I don't want any tea, Aunt Liz. I don't want anything from you except to get you out of my life once and for all!"

The sharpness of her niece's words stung Liz to the core. "Pat? I don't understand . . ."

"How dare you tell John about Marianne!"

Liz looked at Pat, surprised. "You mean you knew about the abortion?"

"Yes, I knew, but Marianne made me promise not to tell her father. Now you've gone and driven the whole family apart."

"Why don't you talk to Barbara Weaver? She's the one who forced Marianne into this abortion!" Liz sputtered. "Can't you see, she knew it would cause trouble between you and John?"

"You're the one who told John, not Barbara," Pat insisted.

"Well, somebody had to! Besides, I didn't think you knew anything about it."

"Well, you'll be happy to know that John left the house tonight for good."

"And you let him?!"

"Thanks to you, Aunt Liz, I really didn't have much choice."

"Barbara Weaver is trying to destroy your marriage and now you're blaming me? How could you? That woman's been after John from the beginning."

"I told you to leave her out of it!"

"When are you going to wise up, Pat? When John starts carrying on with her like he did with Bernice?"

"That's enough, Aunt Liz!"

"He's probably running into her arms right now, just like she planned."

"I said that's enough!"

"How can you be so blind," Liz went on, hoping to scare Pat into fighting for John. "He's made a fool out of you once, and now you're just turning your head all over again."

Pat turned on her heels and made a bee-line for the door. Aunt Liz followed in hot pursuit.

"I'm only telling you this for your own good, Pat."

"You stay out of my life, Aunt Liz," Pat warned menacingly.

"You need somebody to protect your interests," Aunt Liz protested.

"I don't need you, Aunt Liz, not any more."

Liz's expression was one of absolute shock. "What are you saying, Pat?"

"I'm saying that after what you did, I never want to see you again!" Pat flung open the door and raced down the hall of the apartment building. Liz ran out after her, reeling from the pain of Pat's words.

"Pat? Honey, you don't mean that . . ." But Pat was long gone. Liz felt her whole body begin to tremble. Pat was her favorite niece and now she acted like she hated her!

* * *

Soon after Pat left, Liz went over to see Jim. He, however, was not especially pleased to see her, especially since he'd made an evening bridge date. But he also couldn't very well throw her out in her highly charged state.

"You should have heard the awful things Pat said to me," Liz moaned.

"You had no right to interfere, Liz."

"But what about Marianne?"

"If what you say is true, you should have just kept it to yourself and let Pat and John handle it. It was a family matter, Liz, something for them to deal with alone. Why can't you ever get that through your head?"

Liz shook her head in disbelief. "Marianne had an abortion. Don't you realize how serious that is?"

"Yes I do. And when Marianne was ready to tell us about it, she would have."

"The only person she told was that awful Barbara woman. You wouldn't believe me when I told you she was out to break up Pat and John's marriage. What do you say now?"

"The same thing I said before: stay out of it."

Liz angrily buttoned up her coat. "I can see it was a mistake to expect any sympathy from you!"

"If Pat isn't talking to you, you've only got yourself to blame," Jim reminded her as he showed his sister-in-law out the door.

"One of these days, you'll all be sorry you didn't listen to me," Liz warned. "And by then it will probably be too late!"

It seemed an eternity before Pat Randolph's phone rang and Dave Gilchrist was on the other end.

"I'm sorry, Pat. I had an emergency. Rachel Cory was rushed into the hospital."

"Oh no! I hope it's nothing serious," Pat said, forgetting her own problems for a moment.

"We're not sure yet," Dave replied. "We're still doing tests. Now, what can I do for you?"

Pat took a deep breath. She hated to be such a bother, such a crybaby, but Dave had been such an indulgent listener. By now, she had come to really depend on him.

"John found out about Marianne," she said flatly.

"What do you mean by 'found out'? Didn't Marianne tell him?"

"I'm afraid not. Aunt Liz overheard Marianne talking about the abortion to John's partner, Barbara Weaver. Aunt Liz told John."

"I'm sorry, Pat," Dave said, genuinely concerned. "What was his reaction?"

No matter how she tried to fight it, Pat couldn't keep from bursting into tears. "He walked out on me," she sobbed.

"Oh, Pat!"

"You should have seen the way he looked at me, Dave. It was awful."

Dave felt a wave of longing wash over him. Although he tried to fight it, Pat Randolph affected him in a very big way. Somehow, he felt responsible for her happiness, and the sound of her voice—so pained, so despairing —practically tore him apart.

"I'm on call tonight, Pat, but I can come right over if you really need me?" he offered, hoping against hope that she would take him up on his offer.

"Oh, Dave, I'd be so grateful," she whispered, wiping away her tears.

"I'll be over as soon as I can get away."

Pat hung up the phone and felt an enormous sense of relief. *Thank God for Dave,* she told herself. Thirty minutes later, the doorbell rang. Pat opened the door and immediately started crying again as Dave stepped into the foyer. Instinctively, he took her in his arms and held her for several minutes, until her tears stopped.

143

"I'm so sorry about all this," Pat began. "I have no right to be involving you. It's just that—"

"I wouldn't be here if I didn't want to be involved," Dave assured her as he walked her into the parlor. *And just how involved am I?* he asked himself. Probably far more than he was willing to admit, he guessed.

"John said the most terrible things. He said that I never wanted to marry him, that I only did because he got me off the hook for Tom Baxter's murder."

"He's probably just hurt, Pat. You know people say a lot of things they don't mean when they're in pain."

Pat shook her head in disagreement. "He meant them all right. The thing is, I'm not sure whether he's right or not."

Dave studied her for a moment. "What does that mean?"

"I don't know." She paced the room anxiously, running her long fingers through her straight blond hair. "John is a wonderful man. He's been a terrific father and a good husband for the most part. But I was only a teenager when we got married."

Dave understood what Pat was trying to say, and it troubled him. Her confusion mirrored his own. On the one hand, he was well aware that he was attracted to Pat, but he had done his best to suppress that in case she wanted to save her marriage. On the other hand, if she wasn't really happy with John and perhaps hadn't been for quite some time, there was nothing wrong with letting her know how he felt. Not all at once, of course. But in time, after she'd had a while to sort things out.

"Do you think this business with Marianne was just sort of a catalyst?" he found himself asking, for his own personal, though not totally selfish reasons.

"I'm just not sure, Dave. I don't know what I feel anymore," Pat replied, very distraught.

"Do you know where John is now?"

Pat shook her head. "I just hope he hasn't gone and done

anything foolish. He took off like a shot, and if anything happened to him, I couldn't live with myself!"

Dave walked over and put a comforting arm around Pat's shoulder. "I wish I could do something to make this easier on you," he said with deep warmth.

"You have, Dave. You've been here, you've listened to me. I don't know what I would have done without you!"

Dave took Pat in his arms, holding her gently as she cried softly on his shoulder. His impulse was to kiss the tears off her face, but his better judgment told him not to. If Pat and John found they could not work out their difficulties, there would be time enough then for him to tell Pat how he really felt.

"It's going to be all right, Pat," he whispered.

Pat just burrowed her head deeper into his shoulder. "I don't know what to do, Dave."

"I'm going to help you, Pat. I promise. The worst is over. You'll see."

From the other end of the room, Marianne Randolph stood, unnoticed, watching in horror as her mother rested in Dave Gilchrist's arms. She felt her lips trembling and wanted to scream. This was all her doing! She had practically pushed Dave and Pat together because of her own problems. There was only one solution. Marianne had to speak to her father, tonight!

Chapter Ten
Touch and Go

Marianne Randolph headed to the only place she could think her father would go in a time of distress: his office on Sycamore Street. It seemed to be his haven away from the rest of the world, a place where he felt truly in control of his life. Marianne, unfortunately, did not feel the same way. As she stepped in the elevator and pressed the button for the seventh floor, her heart skipped a beat. Small beads of perspiration broke out on her forehead. How was she ever going to face him? she wondered. What could she possibly say that would make him forgive her? Barbara had been right, as had her mother and Michael. She should have confided in her father from the beginning. It was doubly hard having to tell him the truth now.

She walked into the darkened offices tentatively.

"Is anybody here?" she called out, her voice barely above a whisper. There was no answer. Marianne breathed a sigh of relief. Perhaps her father wasn't there after all, and she wouldn't have to face him, at least not tonight. But then she noticed the narrow stream of yellow light under his door. He was there all right. She couldn't turn back now, not if she wanted to see her parents together again and happy, the way they were before she made her mother the guardian of her terrible secret.

Marianne knocked on the door lightly. There was no answer. Slowly, she turned the knob and opened the door a crack. She saw the back of her father's chair and the top of his head, which faced the window. On his desk there was a bottle of whiskey and a half-full glass. Tears formed in Marianne's eyes. What had she done? It was a long time before she found her voice and called out to her father.

"Daddy . . . it's me, Marianne," she said softly.

John did not turn. His face remained hardened as he sat in his chair, staring blankly out the window. Marianne walked around to face him.

"I'm sorry, Daddy," she cried. "I never meant to hurt anybody. I just didn't want you to be disappointed in me."

John straightened up and met his daughter's gaze. "You aren't a disappointment to me," he said in a steely voice. "You're not even my daughter. My daughter wouldn't run off and do such a thing without even discussing it with her parents."

"I couldn't tell you, don't you see? After all the times you warned me about Chris, how could I possibly tell you I was pregnant?"

John was not moved one bit. "What you did is unforgiveable and now you're telling me the reason you did it was because you were a coward!"

"Please, Daddy, please don't be mad at me," she begged, kneeling at his feet and putting her head on his knees.

Though John ached to the core of his being to comfort his precious daughter, he couldn't. Obviously she had no more regard for his feelings than anyone else in the family, and for that he felt totally betrayed. That his own daughter had confided in Barbara, a virtual stranger, and not her own father, absolutely boggled his mind. In one giant stroke, everything had fallen apart: his family, his marriage, everything that mattered to him in the world.

"I'm not interested in what you have to say, Marianne," he said sternly.

"But, Daddy, you haven't even listened to me."

"I know all I need to know. You didn't trust me; you and your mother went behind my back and made a decision that should have been a family decision without even consulting me."

Tears were streaming down Marianne's cheeks. "I was afraid to tell you, Daddy. You've got to believe that!"

"That's a lie and you know it! I've never given you any reason to be afraid to tell me anything. I would have been able to help you. You would have made me feel like I mattered to you. Now I know I don't. Not to you, not to your mother."

"That's not true. Mom loves you. She only asked Dr. Gilchrist to go to New York with her because she couldn't tell you."

John gazed back at his daughter with a wounded look. "Dave Gilchrist went to New York with Pat?"

"She just didn't know who else to turn to, I guess. But there's nothing more to it than that, I promise." Immediately, Marianne knew that she had said too much. She suddenly realized that John had no idea that Dave had accompanied Pat to New York.

"Dave Gilchrist went to New York with her?" he repeated half-aloud, trying to absorb it all.

"It's only because he's my doctor," she tried to explain, but John wasn't listening anymore.

"Go home, Marianne. It's getting late."

"But what about you?"

"I said go home," he repeated firmly. Marianne tried to protest, but John cut her off. "I have nothing more to say to you, do you understand? Now leave me alone!"

Marianne stared at her father for a long moment, then whirled around and ran out of the office. He listened as the sound of her footsteps disappeared down the long hallway. Grasping the glass of whiskey sitting on his desk, he held it firmly between his hands until his knuckles turned white. Then he downed it in one swallow, and brought the glass down hard on his desk. "She and Dave Gilchrist were in New York together," he spat out.

Marianne ran past the elevator and straight down the seven flights of stairs, trying to contain her sobs. But it was useless. In the lobby, she went over to the public phone and dialed Barbara's number.

"I've never seen Daddy so torn up," she cried when Barbara answered. "I'm afraid he might do something to hurt himself!"

"Marianne, I want you to listen to me," came Barbara's calm, logical voice. "Go home. I'm leaving now. I'll take care of John."

"What about my mother?"

"Just tell her I'm going to the office to talk to him. I'll try to convince him to go home. I'll call you later and let you know what happens. Are you calm enough to drive, Marianne?"

Marianne suddenly felt a million times better. Barbara had a way of taking charge that gave her the sense that everything would be fine if she just followed her directives. "I'm fine, Barbara. And thanks, you're a good friend."

Fifteen minutes later, Barbara walked into John's office. The first thing she did was take the bottle of whiskey away from him.

"This isn't going to help anything!" she said in her typically no-nonsense way. But John wasn't particularly glad to see her.

"You all must take me for the fool of the century!" he said, forcing a laugh.

"If you believe that, maybe you are!" she shot back.

"Look, this is no time to start feeling sorry for yourself. Your daughter got pregnant. She had an abortion. Those are the facts, counselor, and you've got to come to grips with them. Forget about how disappointed you are and think about Marianne. She was terrified. She wanted to tell you, but she couldn't."

John turned toward her, his eyes filled with outrage. "Did you tell her to have the abortion?"

"You know me better than that. I told you, I advised Marianne to discuss it with her parents."

"But you don't see anything particularly wrong with what she did, do you?"

"What I think doesn't matter. It was Marianne's decision."

John flew off the handle. "She's only eighteen, for God's sake! What kind of an informed decision can someone so young make?"

"Marianne is not a child. Maybe if you started realizing that, she wouldn't be afraid to tell you things."

"Get out of here!" he said, more angry at himself than at Barbara.

"Not without you," she replied, standing up to him. "Let me take you home."

John shook his head. "I'm not going back there," he said vehemently. "I'll stay at a hotel."

"Fine, I'll drive you there." Barbara got his coat from the closet. "Coming?"

Alice took Beatrice's coat and led her into the living room. Ever since Beatrice had called her an hour earlier, Alice had been sitting on pins and needles. *She's made a decision,* Alice thought, watching the woman's serious expression.

"I wanted to come over and tell you that I've given all our talks very serious consideration," Beatrice began.

Alice swallowed hard. This wasn't getting off to a good

start at all, she thought. "What have you decided to do, Beatrice?" Alice asked, figuring there was no sense in prolonging this any more than was necessary.

"Is Sally at home?"

"She's upstairs doing her homework," Alice replied, her stomach tightening.

Beatrice folded her hands in her lap. "I love Sally very much. I know you do, too."

"There's no reason why we both can't love her," Alice volunteered.

Beatrice smiled. "I believe you mean that, Alice."

"I do, with all my heart. I think it's very important for Sally to have a grandmother."

"So do I. That's why I've decided to drop my custody suit and just be her grandmother, if that's all right with you?"

Alice gasped. "Oh, Beatrice, thank you! Thank you from the bottom of my heart!" She threw her arms around the older woman and they both began to cry.

"I know you'll be a good mother to Sally," Beatrice said, taking out a tissue and wiping her eyes. "The two of you are so good together. I always used to say that before . . ."

"I remember," Alice said, smiling through her tears.

"I want you to know that it was never my intention to hurt you, Alice."

"I know that," she assured her.

"It's just that I thought I could make everything up to Jenny by raising Sally. But I can't ever do that. I had my chance once and I lost it."

Alice touched her arm gently. "It's over now, Beatrice. I think you should just try to be happy to watch Jenny's child grow up. Sit back and be a doting grandmother, what do you say?"

"It sounds wonderful!"

Alice smiled with gratitude. "There's just one piece of business we ought to take care of."

"What's that?" Beatrice asked.

"I think it's about time Sally met her grandmother!"

Iris was in her sitting room, touching up her nail polish, when Tracey entered carrying a coffee tray.

"Louise asked me to bring this in," she said in a dull tone.

"Wonderful," Iris cooed. "I'm just in the mood for another cup of coffee."

Tracey had known Iris for a long time, but even she was taken aback by her friend's lack of compassion. "Don't you think you should go to the hospital?" she asked at last.

"Whatever for? I'm sure Rachel's just faking the whole thing to get Daddy's attention."

"If that were the case, they would have discharged her, Iris. You really ought to go over there. Mac is probably a wreck."

"I am not about to go running down to the hospital at this hour," Iris said, continuing to polish her nails.

Tracey was appalled. "How can you be indifferent to something that's causing Mac so much pain?"

"I don't understand you, Tracey. I thought you cared about Daddy."

"I do, too much not to respect his love for Rachel."

"I already told you—" Iris began.

"You're wrong about that, dead wrong. Mac is very much in love with Rachel, and if you don't believe that, you are a bigger fool than I was for thinking I could get back my old summer romance." Tracey put down the tray and headed for the door.

"Tracey, wait, please," Iris entreated. "I suppose you're right. I really should go over to the hospital. Would you come with me?"

Tracey eyed her friend with confusion. "Whatever for, Iris? It's hardly my place to be there."

"Call it moral support, darling. If Rachel starts jabbering to Daddy about her phone calls, I'm afraid I'm going to need a friend."

Mac was sitting forlornly on a bench in the waiting room when Ada came over with a cup of hot coffee.

"If you're planning to sit up here all night, you had better be prepared," she said, handing him the styrofoam cup. "It's only hospital cafeteria coffee, but it'll do the job."

Mac took the cup between his hands. "Thank you, Ada. I don't know what I'd do without you at times like this."

"You'd do just fine," she assured him.

"What's taking them so long?" Mac bristled. "We should have been able to see Rachel by now."

"Russ is in with her. Just give them a chance to see what's wrong."

"The longer it takes, the more worried I get," Mac said, leaping up from his seat. "I just don't understand it. She seemed fine earlier. How could something like this just happen?"

Ada was about to answer when Russ Matthews came out of the intensive care unit. Mac and Ada were at his side immediately.

"What is it, Russ? How is Rachel? Is she going to lose the baby?"

Russ raised his eyebrows. He knew the prognosis was not good, but he had in a call to Dave Gilchrist for a consultation before anything definite was decided.

"Rachel's had some internal bleeding," Russ told them. "I'm afraid she's very weak right now. Her blood pressure is dangerously elevated and she's got a fever."

Mac looked like he had been hit by a ton of bricks.

"It sounds pretty bad, Russ. Just level with me, is Rachel's life in danger?"

"No, Mac, not at the moment. But I won't kid you. Her condition is serious. I think she may need surgery."

"Can we see her, Russ?" Ada asked, the fear finally beginning to show on her face.

"She's not conscious, but you can each go in and spend a minute or two with her. No more, though. I'll check back with you after I've spoken to Dave."

Ada and Mac stared at each other, unable to say a word.

"Go on inside, Mac. I'm sure Rachel would want you to be there."

Mac squeezed Ada's hand. "Thank you, Ada," he replied gratefully and disappeared inside the ICU. Ada took a deep breath. She had been through a lot of rough times with Rachel, but never had she been as scared as she was this time.

As Mac stood at Rachel's bedside, tears came into his eyes. Why had he gone to Iris's? If he had been home with his wife as he should have been, maybe none of this would have happened. But what Mac couldn't understand as he looked down on Rachel's pale, emotionless face, was why she hadn't called him at Iris's if she wasn't feeling well? Why would she take a chance, especially with the baby on the way?

Sitting by her bedside, Mac took his wife's limp hand in his. "Please come back to me, Rachel," he whispered. "I love you so much!"

Mac gazed at his wife tenderly. She looked so peaceful and beautiful, as if she were sleeping. Mac remembered how happy he'd been when Rachel came into his life; he had been alone for a long time after the death of Iris's mother. Although he was no stranger to the jet-set party circuit, he had counted himself a very lonely man. Then he came to Bay City and everything changed. Rachel Frame had walked into his life, young and sassy as a spring breeze, and made him laugh again. She made him feel like a boy practically from the first moment he laid eyes on her.

Gently, he stroked her long, dark hair, thinking that even now, as sick as she was, Rachel was still the most beautiful woman he'd ever seen. His heart felt sick at the thought that he could possibly lose her. All his money, all his power, would have meant nothing without Rachel. She was his true riches, and he never doubted that for one minute.

Suddenly Mac felt a hand on his shoulder. He turned and saw Dave Gilchrist standing there.

"Dave, have you spoken with Russ yet?" he asked, anxiously.

"Russ and I just went over the options, Mac. We may have to operate."

"When would you do it?"

"We're going to watch Rachel's condition for the rest of the night and see if we can get her stabilized. Right now her blood pressure is still too high to consider surgery."

"I don't understand this, Dave. She was fine all day long. We had lunch together. She was happy and laughing. What could have gone wrong?"

Dave knitted his brows. "Has Rachel been under any kind of stress lately?"

Mac thought of the situation with Beatrice Gordon and frowned. "Well, she has become rather heavily involved in our housekeeper's problems. I'm afraid we've had some angry words about it a few times.

"I'm not saying that's what did it, but you could say that Rachel's suffering from a kind of chain reaction in her body. The elevated blood pressure triggered bleeding in the amniotic sac. She was probably in a lot of pain. I'm surprised she didn't call someone," Dave said, echoing Mac's own puzzlement.

"I tried to call the house from my daughter's place and the line was busy. She was probably trying to reach me when she collapsed and the phone got knocked over."

155

Dave looked troubled. "Then you have no idea how long she was unconscious?"

Mac felt his chest tighten. "She spoke to Ada several hours before I found her. I suppose it could've been anywhere from a few minutes to a few hours."

"That could be a problem," Dave commented. "The more bleeding in the amniotic sac, the less likely it is that we'll be able to prevent a miscarriage."

"If Rachel loses the baby, she'll be heartbroken," Mac said sadly.

"We'll do the best we can. Why don't you go home, and come back in the morning. There's not much you can do here tonight."

"I couldn't leave, Dave. Not when Rachel's condition is so tenuous."

Dave smiled compassionately. "I'll have the floor nurse fix you up a room down the hall."

"Thank you, but I don't think I'll be getting much sleep."

Mac went outside while Dave remained to check Rachel's vital signs. Ada walked up to him.

"Well, what did Dave have to say?"

"They might have to operate," Mac replied, clearly upset.

"What about the baby?"

Mac shook his head. "They don't know, Ada, but it doesn't look good."

As they headed for the waiting area, they saw Iris and Tracey come in. Tracey looked slightly embarrassed.

"Daddy we came as soon as we heard," Iris said, hugging her father with practiced sincerity. "Tracey insisted on coming along," she added, only causing her friend further embarrassment. Ada leveled both women with a menacing look. Only hours earlier, Rachel had confided to her mother that Iris was at it again, trying to woo Mac away from her with Tracey. But as Ada studied Tracey, she felt certain that the woman posed no threat.

"Tracey DeWitt, this is Rachel's mother, Ada McGowen," Mac said, making the introductions.

"I'm so sorry to hear about Rachel, Mrs. McGowen," Tracey said honestly.

"Thank you. I've heard a lot about you, Mrs. DeWitt. It is Mrs. isn't it?"

"Yes, it is," Tracey replied, taking her meaning immediately.

Ada turned to Iris. "I'm surprised to see you here, Iris."

"Honestly, Ada, I would hardly have left Daddy to go through this alone. Tracey tried to tell me to stay home, but I just couldn't!"

Tracey shot her friend a look of sheer incredulity, which Ada noticed. "I'll just bet," she said, figuring that Iris had dragged Tracey along to make one last shot at Mac while Rachel was flat on her back and unable to defend herself. *Well*, Ada thought, *I'll keep an eye on them for her.*

"Has Rachel told you what happened?" Iris asked, hoping to find out if Rachel had spilled the beans about her hanging up on her twice.

"She hasn't regained consciousness yet," Mac said, shaking his head.

"Oh, how dreadful," Iris remarked, though breathing an inward sigh of relief. At least Rachel hadn't had a chance to poison Mac's mind against her yet. Iris would just have to make sure that she never did.

Moments later when Mac and Ada decided to go down to the cafeteria for some dinner, Iris saw her opportunity to get into Rachel's room.

"What are you going to do?" Tracey asked, not willing to put anything past her friend at this point.

"I'm going to make sure that that little witch doesn't go running off at the mouth to Daddy!"

Tracey grabbed Iris by the coat sleeve. "You heard Mac; she's unconscious!"

"Well, then, I'll just have to wake her up, won't I?" She pulled away and made a bee-line for the ICU. But no sooner had Iris approached the door than Russ Matthews blocked her path.

"Where do you think you're going?" he asked, not at all happy to see his one-time fiancée.

"I want to see Rachel, of course."

"Sorry, Iris, she can't have any visitors, especially not you."

Iris raised her chin defiantly. "Since when have you become Rachel's defender?"

"Get out of here, Iris, before I say something we'll both regret," Russ warned.

But she wasn't about to be put off. "You of all people should recognize an act when you see one. Rachel surely pulled enough of them on you!"

Russ's blood began to boil. It was true that he and Rachel hadn't been on good terms for a long time after their divorce, but they had both since come to terms with their youthful follies and had even become friends. The Rachel lying so helplessly on the bed in the ICU was a very different woman from the selfish and manipulative young girl he'd married years ago, and as her friend he was not about to let Iris stand there and malign her.

"If you don't get out of here right now, I will physically throw you out."

Iris put her hands on her hips. "I have a perfect right to be here and you know it!" she said, raising her voice.

"In case you haven't noticed, this is a hospital. I won't have you causing a scene."

"If you don't get out of my way, you're going to see a scene they'll be talking about in this dreary town for years!" she cried.

158

With that, Russ took her roughly by the arm and started to walk her down the corridor, Iris fighting and struggling the whole way.

"Let go of me!" she bellowed.

Just then, Mac came running around the corner. "What is going on!" he demanded to know, casting an angry glare at Iris.

"Mac, I want you to get your daughter out of here. I don't want her anywhere near Rachel's room. The last thing Rachel needs right now is to be put under greater stress!"

"What were you doing by Rachel's room?" Mac demanded sternly.

"I just wanted to see how she was," Iris replied in an innocent voice.

"She was making a scene, Mac, and I won't have it. Rachel's room is off limits to Iris, is that clear?" Russ asked, looking her straight in the eye.

Mac tried his best to contain his anger. "Go home, Iris," he instructed her.

"But, Daddy . . ."

"Go home and don't come back here," he ordered, just barely holding on to his temper.

"I can't do anything right, can I?" she pouted. "Ever since you married Rachel, no matter how hard I try, you find a way to put me in the wrong!"

Mac looked at Tracey, who appeared to be mortified, to say the least.

"Will you please get Iris out of here?" he asked.

"How can you treat me like this?" Iris protested as Tracey took her by the arm.

"I have too many things on my mind right now to worry about your feelings, Iris. I won't say this again: go home. If you care for me at all, just leave me alone." Mac turned his back on her and walked down the long corridor toward

Rachel's room. Iris started to go after him, but Tracey stopped her.

"You'll only make it worse, Iris," her friend advised. "Mac is under a terrible strain right now. Don't add to it."

Reluctantly, Iris followed her friend to the elevator. If she couldn't see Rachel tonight, she would make damn sure she did in the morning. She could not risk having Rachel tell Mac about the phone calls. If she did, Iris was certain she would lose her father—maybe forever.

Mac was slumped, half-asleep on a chair outside the ICU when Dave Gilchrist shook him gently early the next morning. Mac awakened with a start.

"Is it Rachel? Has anything happened?"

"I've got the results of the rest of the tests, Mac. I'm afraid we can't put surgery off any longer . . ."

Chapter Eleven
Confessions

Feeling sick at heart that John hadn't come home after storming out of the house the night before, Pat swallowed her pride and called his office. Barbara answered.

"May I speak with John, please?" Pat asked, dispensing with the usually, obligatory chit-chat.

"Is that you, Pat?" Barbara queried, herself a bit embarrassed.

"Yes," she replied flatly.

"I'm afraid John hasn't come in yet," Barbara informed her, feeling very much caught in the middle.

Pat tried to hold her voice steady, but her spirits, in fact all of her self-esteem, was plummeting to an all-time low. If Barbara hadn't known before that John had not spent the night with his wife, she surely knew now, Pat thought. But then again, this was no time for worrying what people thought. The important thing was to find out where John was.

"You wouldn't happen to know where he is?" Pat asked, her voice almost a whisper.

Barbara was not sure what to do. If John wanted Pat to know where he was staying, surely he would have told her himself. But Barbara did not want to help widen the chasm between them by lying to Pat. She decided to play it loose for the time being and see what developed.

"I know John will be in very shortly. He called from Judge Hawthorne's chambers about ten minutes ago and said he was on his way," she lied. There, that didn't sound so bad, Barbara told herself. It wasn't exactly the truth, but it didn't embarrass Pat unnecessarily either. She could tell John's wife was grateful.

"Well then, I'll call him back later," Pat said, her voice somewhat uplifted.

"His calendar's free after two thirty," Barbara offered. "Why not stop over?"

"Thank you. I might just do that," Pat said. She hung up the phone slowly and breathed a sigh of relief. She had been prepared to hear a whole litany of nasty accusations from John, and now at least she had a few hours reprieve. How much did Barbara know? she wondered again. The woman was certainly being exceeding solicitous, even warm. Maybe Pat might be able to use her as an ally, she thought. Surely Barbara had some influence with John.

But no sooner had the thought crossed her mind than Pat stopped herself. What had happened was between herself and John alone. They had to work through it by themselves, if that was even possible. Most importantly, they had to sit down and have an honest talk, which wasn't going to be easy. She wasn't sure why or how, but this experience with Marianne had somehow stirred up a whole cauldron of bitterness. Perhaps deep down, Pat had never really forgiven John for his affair with Bernice years ago. Maybe since the day she'd found out about it, they had just been moving further and further apart. Whatever the reason, Pat knew that too much had been left unsaid between them, and it had to be said now. If John wouldn't come to her, she would have to go to him.

Later that afternoon, she appeared at her husband's

office. Apparently Barbara had not told John of their conversation earlier, so he was taken by complete surprise by his wife's visit.

"Don't you think we should talk about this?" Pat began, ready to lay her soul bare if necessary.

"I don't think there's much to talk about, Pat," John replied coldly, barely looking at her.

"We've got to talk. You can't just walk out of the house and leave it at that."

"I think that's what you wanted all along. Now you can go and cry some more on Dave Gilchrist's shoulder." Pat was taken aback at the mention of her friend's name. "I guess he was another one of your little secrets," John accused.

"Dave Gilchrist is a friend. He's Marianne's doctor and if it hadn't been for his support, these last few weeks would have been even more painful and confusing," Pat blurted out.

"You didn't want me to come to New York with you because of him!"

"I didn't want to hurt you, John. I thought if Marianne hadn't already had the abortion, there would be no reason to tell you anything. You would have never had to know. But I needed someone. So, I asked Dave to come along."

John listened, but Pat could see he wasn't about to change his position.

"You betrayed me, every one of you. Look at it however you like, the truth of the matter is that I was treated like an outsider and Dave Gilchrist, who really is a stranger, was taken into the bosom of family confidence. How do you expect me to react to that?"

"I might say the same thing about you and Barbara," Pat shot back.

"There's no comparison and you know it!"

"Oh, no?" Pat asked. Then she took a deep breath. "The point is, John, that no one was shutting you out.

All any of us wanted to do was spare your feelings. When I found Marianne in that clinic in New York, I begged her to tell you about the abortion, but she out and out refused."

"Then it was your duty to come to me," John insisted.

"I couldn't. I gave Marianne my word," Pat replied weakly. "I didn't feel I could break her trust."

John paced back and forth, trying to understand his wife's motivations, but try as he did, only one thing seemed clear: Pat did not love him anymore, if in fact she ever had. "Michael and Marianne are the only ones you've ever really cared about," he said bluntly.

Pat stared at him in disbelief. "Of course I care about them. They're my children, our children. How can you be jealous of your own flesh and blood?"

It was as though John hadn't heard a word she'd said. "You never cared about me, Pat! Do you think my affair with Bernice Kline would have ever happened if you had?"

The reality of his words stung Pat to the core. Often over the years, she'd asked herself that very same question. If she had been a really good wife to John, would he have ever gotten involved with another woman? Even now, she didn't want to dwell on it long enough to formulate an answer.

"I would like you to come home, John, so we can talk about things in a more civilized manner," she said, firmly.

"I can't, Pat. I don't know what I'm going to do, but I can't come home."

"You can't just walk out," she said in amazement.

"I'll talk to Michael and Marianne, if that's what you're worried about."

"What about me? Do I get the same courtesy?" she demanded, feeling angry all of a sudden.

"I'll call you, Pat," John replied, looking out his window and all but dismissing her.

Pat's head began to throb at the temples. *It's all over*, she told herself. *He isn't coming back.* The most troubling thing about it was that she wasn't sure whether she cared or not.

Dave Gilchrist was concerned when Pat called him that afternoon, practically in tears.

"I tried to talk to John, but it was no use," she said softly. "He thinks I've betrayed him. He says I never loved him at all."

"I have a couple of hours off," Dave told her. "Why don't I come over and we can talk?"

Immediately, Pat felt her whole body relax. She didn't know what it was, but just having Dave to talk to seemed to make everything better. It gave her a whole new perspective on things. She was aware, of course, that she had come to depend on him perhaps too heavily. And each time she dialed his number, she would tell herself that it was for just this one last time. But invariably, she'd end up calling him the next time she felt things closing in on her. Dave didn't seem to mind, either.

"I don't know what I feel anymore, Dave," she told him later, as she poured them some tea. "I've been married to John since I was Marianne's age. I don't know any other life but being married to him. Sometimes I think all this business with Marianne has forced us to confront real problems in our marriage, and then I wonder if I'm just overreacting."

Dave took Pat's hands between his, reassuring her. "I can't answer questions about the state of your marriage, Pat. All I know is what I see and you don't look like a very happy lady. I thought it was because of Marianne's problems."

"It is, at least to some extent," Pat covered. "It's just that I think maybe there's something else there too, and I think it has to do with John and me."

Dave looked at her seriously. "Do you want to make your marriage work, Pat?"

"Yes! What else have I got?" she replied, a bit too quickly.

"That's not what I asked you."

There was a long moment of silence as Pat gazed into his penetrating brown eyes. Somehow, she felt sure he knew things, secret things about her that she did not even begin to understand herself.

"Mom, where's Daddy?" Marianne called, barreling into the living room and stopping short at the sight of her mother and Dave Gilchrist holding hands. Immediately, Pat pulled away, her hand shooting to her lap.

"Marianne, you scared me half to death!"

Marianne looked from Pat to Dave. The first time she had caught them together, in each other's arms in that very same living room, Marianne had tried to dismiss it. She'd reasoned that Dr. Gilchrist was a good friend and there was nothing more to it. Now, with this trouble with her father, Marianne was beginning to think there was something more to it.

"Did I interrupt something?" she muttered sarcastically.

"We were just talking about your father," Pat said, embarrassed.

"Daddy didn't come home last night, did he?"

"No, dear," Pat replied, feeling ashamed, "he didn't."

"Well, aren't you going to do something about it? You're not just going to accept it!"

"There's not much I can do, Marianne. It's all up to your father, now."

"This is all because of me, isn't it?" Marianne asked, tears welling up in her eyes.

Pat would have liked to have been able to spare her daughter the guilt, but Dave had been right when he'd said that Marianne should be made to face her own responsibilities.

"You put me in an awful position with your father," Pat said calmly.

"So now you're breaking up? Because of me?"

"I never said that. Your father blames me for not telling him about your pregnancy, and truthfully, Marianne, I don't know what's going to happen next."

Marianne shook her head in disbelief and ran out of the room. Dave squeezed Pat's hand, keeping her from running after her daughter. "She'll be all right. Let her handle this on her own!"

About the only thing Marianne could think to do after driving around town for hours, was to stop at Barbara's apartment. If anyone had any influence with her father at this point, it would have to be Barbara.

"Marianne!" Barbara said, surprised to see her standing in the doorway.

"I've got . . . to talk to you," she stammered. "My whole family's falling apart and it's all my fault!"

Barbara calmed her young friend down by sitting her on the couch and making them some hot chocolate.

"Do you know where Daddy is?" Marianne asked at last.

Barbara bit her lower lip. This had gone too far, she thought. John couldn't cut himself off from his family forever. "He's at the Avery Hotel."

Marianne's face dropped. "They're getting a divorce, aren't they?" she asked, panic evident in her tone.

"I think your father just needs some time by himself to think things out," Barbara replied.

"Would you talk to him, Barbara? I know he'll listen to you."

"I've already told him I think he should talk things out with your mother. I don't know what else I can do."

"Tell him it was all my fault. Please, before it's too late," she pleaded.

"What do you mean, 'too late'?" Barbara asked.

Marianne gulped. "I think my mother's already started seeing someone else," she said slowly.

Barbara stared at Marianne in shock. "You mean another man?"

"Yes. I think Mom's seeing Dr. Gilchrist."

Alice Frame took pains to make sure the dinner she had prepared came out just right. It was the first real "family" dinner she had prepared for Sally since Beatrice had dropped the custody suit. In fact, Beatrice was supposed to have joined them, but that Jim Matthews had surprised her with theater tickets at the last minute. So, it was just going to be the three of them: Alice, Sally and her Uncle Ray.

"I hope you like pot roast," Alice said, taking Ray's coat.

"It's one of my favorites," Ray replied, still feeling a bit awkward in her presence. In fact, he had done his best to avoid Alice after that night he'd come by to apologize for kissing her. It had been difficult, to say the least. But he knew that if he continued to bask in her warm and glowing presence, he would never be able to tear himself away. For that reason, he had arranged for his return to California before he went over to the Frame house.

"I can't wait to meet my two cousins!" Sally said exuberantly over dinner. "Do you think they can come out to Bay City this summer?"

Ray looked at Alice and smiled warmly. "I think we might be able to arrange that, Sally. If Alice wouldn't mind putting up some of the Gordons, that is."

"Are you kidding? The more the merrier." Then she added quickly, "Of course, you'll have to bring Olive, too."

"Olive's pretty fond of her California sunshine," Ray replied. "I don't think anything short of an earthquake would get her to leave."

"Well, you can come by yourself, can't you, Uncle Ray?" Sally prompted. "We have lots of room, right, Alice?"

Alice looked at Ray, embarrassed. "Yes . . . of course."

After dessert, Sally excused herself. "I've got to finish making my product map for social studies," she said, giving Ray a big hug and a kiss.

"You be sure to write to your old uncle, you hear?" Ray said warmly.

"You bet!"

Alice got up. "How about if I tuck you in later?"

"Well, maybe. But I'm not a baby anymore, you know!"

"Well excuse me," Alice said with a light laugh.

Sally gave her mother a kiss. "You're excused." Ray and Alice watched as she skipped up the stairs.

"She's a terrific little girl," Ray said.

"Yes. A little girl who's going on forty!" Alice teased.

In the living room, she poured them each a brandy as Ray put another log on the fire. He turned to Alice. The soft, warm light of the fire cast a glow on her face, and her golden hair shone like gold.

"When will you be leaving Bay City?" she asked, her voice low as she stared into the flames.

"Tomorrow morning," Ray replied.

Alice turned to him, looking as though she had just been wounded. "I thought you'd be here another day or two."

"There's not really much point. My mother's dropped the custody action, and Sally should be your legal daughter by the end of the month."

"I'm sorry," Alice apologized. "I was just being selfish. You must miss your family terribly. I know if I were Olive, I'd hate to have you away for so long. . . ."

Ray held her gaze for what seemed an eternity. "Would you really, Alice?"

Alice felt her face flush. "Any woman would," she replied quickly.

Ray shrugged and stood up to leave. Alice helped him with his coat.

"Thank you, Ray, for everything. Sally and I will never forget what you did for us."

"And I'll never forget you . . . or Sally."

They looked at each other for a long moment, and Alice could feel her heartbeat quickening.

"Good-bye, Alice," Ray said, having obvious difficuly finding the right words.

"Good-bye, Raymond. And good luck." Before she knew what was happening, Ray leaned down to kiss her. His lips were warm and seductive on her mouth. But in a moment, it was over.

"Take care of yourself, Alice," he said, stroking her cheek.

"Don't be a stranger," she heard herself say.

"Don't you worry. I won't."

She watched, mesmerized, as he walked down the driveway and got into his rented car. Seconds later, Ray was out of Alice's life as quickly and as mysteriously as he had entered it. Yet somehow she felt that he was not finished with her, nor she with him. Not yet, and most definitely, not now.

Mac could hardly sleep a wink after Dave told him that Rachel would need surgery. Throughout the night, they waited to see if the medication would lower her blood pressure enough so they could proceed with the operation without endangering her life any more than necessary. At quarter past eight the next morning, Dave and Russ entered Rachel's room, where Mac, his face weary and unshaven, kept his lonely vigil.

"I've scheduled surgery for ten o'clock, Mac," Dave told him. "Russ will be assisting and monitoring the fetal heart rate."

Mac ran his fingers through his salt-and-pepper-gray hair. "Isn't there any way we could avoid surgery?"

"I'm afraid not. The fetus can't stand much more trauma and Rachel's pretty weak herself. We've got to go in there and repair the damage, if we can," Dave advised.

"You mean there's a chance you won't be able to do anything?" Mac asked, suddenly growing white with panic.

"There's always that chance with any surgery," Russ said, "but Rachel's a strong woman."

It was what they weren't saying that bothered Mac the most, and there was no way he would let either doctor get away without laying all the cards on the table.

"Are you telling me that Rachel might not pull through this?"

Dave and Russ exchanged worried looks. "As I said, Rachel's very strong. She's also young, and that's certainly in her favor," Russ said, trying his best to reassure him.

"But something could go wrong," Mac pressed.

Dave looked him straight in the eye. "There's always that possibility. The main thing is that we get in there and fast now that her pressure's down to a decent level."

Russ put his hand on Mac's shoulder. "Why don't you go downstairs and get some breakfast?"

"Can I sit with Rachel for a moment first?" he asked, tears beginning to form in his eyes.

Russ nodded compassionately. "Just for a minute. She's got to be prepped."

Mac shook his head and dragged himself back into the room. Russ watched from the one-way window as he sat beside Rachel's bed. It was incredible how much he loved her, Russ thought. It was even more incredible to him how much Rachel had changed; she was no longer the selfish, materialistic young woman he had known years before when they were married. Mac and Rachel were so right together, and now all of that was at stake. Poor Mac, he thought, grateful that he was not in his position this time. Russ knew better than anyone what it was like to lose a loved one. He had been all through that with his sweet wife, Cindy, and watching Mac leaning over Rachel's bed brought it all back.

Inside the ICU, Mac held Rachel's hand tenderly. She had not opened her eyes once since she was brought in hours earlier. It seemed like an eternity. If she had only spoken to him; if only there was some sign of life. But there was nothing, and it was all his fault. If he had been home where he belonged instead of wasting time at Iris's, perhaps he could have gotten her to the hospital before too much damage was done. Now Rachel's life was on the line, as was the life of their unborn child.

"Please don't leave me, Rachel," he whispered softly. "I can't make it without you, darling." He stroked her hair gently. "We have such a wonderful life ahead of us—you, me and the baby. You can't give up on that. Please, darling, come back to me!"

When Mac finally left the ICU, he saw Ada and Gil waiting outside, their faces serious.

"They're taking her down to surgery soon," Mac said.

"Rachel's going to pull through, do you hear me, Mac?" Ada said firmly, giving him a good shot of positive thinking.

Mac smiled, grateful. "You bet she will, Ada," he agreed.

Soon after that, Rachel was wheeled out of the ICU. Mac followed the gurney down to the operating room, where Dave was waiting.

"This will probably take several hours, Mac."

"Dave, there's something I want you to understand," Mac said. "If it comes to a choice between Rachel and the baby . . ." His voice began to crack.

"Let's not anticipate the worst, okay?"

"I'm not, but if it does come to a choice, I want you to save my wife."

Dave put his hand on Mac's shoulder, and then disappeared behind the forbidding gray doors of the OR.

Three hours later, the doors swung open. Dave, still in his surgical greens, came out, followed by Russ. Mac spotted them from down the hall in the waiting room. He got up slowly, measuring their expressions as they approached. Ada and Gil got up next. Instinctively, Ada's hand clutched her chest.

"Rachel is fine . . ." Dave began cautiously.

"The surgery turned out to be more delicate than we had anticipated at first," Russ went on.

Mac's face was jubilant. "Thank God!" he cried. "Thank you, Russ, Dave. Thank you for giving my Rachel back to me!"

"What about the baby?" Ada asked, looking at them and realizing that something was not right. There was a moment of silence as Russ and Dave struggled for the appropriate words.

"The baby's all right, isn't he?" Mac asked.

"I'm sorry, Mac, we couldn't save him," Dave replied softly.

Mac felt his happiness partially drain away. "That baby meant everything to Rachel," he said sadly.

"There was nothing we could do," Russ assured him. "Maybe if we had gotten Rachel here sooner . . ."

Mac shook his head in despair. "It's my fault!"

"Come on, Mac, there's no way you could have foreseen anything like this," Gil said, trying to comfort him.

"The important thing is that Rachel came through," Ada stated, her strength coming through once again. "You two can have other babies."

But Mac was inconsolable. When Rachel was wheeled out of the recovery room into her own private room, Mac again took up the vigil by her side. Tears streamed down his cheeks as he gazed on her pale, sleeping face. She looked a

173

little like one of those Christmas card angels, Mac thought to himself, marveling at her apparent serenity.

"If you hate me for this, Rachel, I'll deserve it," he whispered softly. "I know how much this baby meant to you. It did to me, too. It was a little boy, you know. We would have had a son, darling, if it hadn't been for my stupidity!" He hid his head in his hands and wept openly.

"Mac . . ." came Rachel's weak voice. Mac looked up, wiping the tears from his eyes. Rachel's eyes were closed.

"I'm here, darling. I'm right here," he said, taking her hand.

"Mac . . ." she moaned in her sleep. "Please, come home. . . ."

Just then, Dave came in to check on his patient. Mac got up, his face riddled with worry.

"She was just saying something. It didn't make much sense," Mac said as Rachel began to toss in the bed.

"Mac . . . Come home, Mac, please . . ."

Dave put his hand on her forehead. "Her temperature is up. We've got to make sure secondary infection doesn't set in."

"Mac . . . I need you," Rachel continued to cry.

"What's the matter with her, Dave?"

"It's just the fever, Mac. She's delirious. I'm going to give her an antibiotic, that should help," he said, injecting her. Then Dave walked Mac to the door. "By tonight, we should have a better indication of how she's coming along."

The two men left the room. For a moment, Rachel lay on the bed, very still. Suddenly, a single tear rolled down her pallid cheek. "Please, Iris, get Mac. . . . Tell him to come home," she whimpered in her sleep.

Chapter Twelve
Shattered Dreams

Iris arrived at Bay City General Hospital bright and early the following morning, her arms filled with flowers for Rachel. That was one way to get into her room, Iris thought, admiring her quick wittedness. Mac, however, barred the way.

"Rachel had a difficult night," he told his daughter. "Why don't you give those flowers to the nurse?"

"Don't be silly, Daddy, I'll just put them in water myself and take them in. Rachel might be awake by then."

"I don't want you in there," Mac said seizing his daughter by the arm.

"Why not?"

"Because . . . Rachel lost our baby. She doesn't know yet, and as soon as she awakens, I want to be there to break it to her."

Iris felt a numbness creeping up her spine. If her father ever found out about Rachel's call now, it really would be the end for her. Wasn't it just like Rachel to cause all this trouble, she thought angrily.

"I'm so sorry, Daddy," she said, doing her best to

empathize. "But you should have never stayed at my house so long!"

Mac looked at his daughter incredulously. "You're the one who was coaxing me to stay. You even wanted me to stay for dinner, don't you remember?"

"Well, yes, but you were in a better position than I to judge whether or not you could leave Rachel all that time." Perhaps by turning the tables, Iris thought, she might buy a little grace for herself and switch the burden of blame. It seemed to be working as Mac buried his face in his hands, clearly distraught.

"How could I have been so stupid!" he railed.

"Well, I hate to say this, Daddy, but you did seem to be awfully preoccupied with Tracey the other night," Iris observed.

Mac lifted his head and stared at his daughter. "What did you say?"

"Come on, Daddy, it was pretty obvious. You couldn't take your eyes off her."

In an instant, Mac grabbed Iris by the shoulders. His dark eyes were wild with rage. "How dare you suggest a thing like that!"

"Daddy, please," Iris squirmed. "I only told you what I saw."

"As always, Iris, you saw what you wanted to see."

"Tracey noticed it, too. She even asked me about it after you left," Iris lied.

"I don't care what you or Tracey think you saw or noticed. The only woman I care about is Rachel! Is that clear!"

"Whatever you say, Daddy," Iris replied, a bit frightened. She had never seen her father so angry before and especially at her. This was all Rachel's fault.

"I want you out of this hospital and I never want to see you near Rachel's room again. Is that understood?"

Iris pouted, and forced little tears into her eyes. "Why are you being so cruel to me, Daddy? I'm not the one who's responsible for Rachel's condition. I even asked her to come over with you!" Well, Iris thought, that was indirectly true, at least. The main thing in her mind was that she had to absolve herself of all blame in Mac's eyes before Rachel blabbed everything to him.

"Just get out of here!" Mac roared. "I mean it, Iris. I don't want to see you here again, and don't get any ideas about dragging Tracey over, either!" Mac spun her around, practically shoving her into the open elevator.

"Daddy . . ." As the doors slid closed in her face, Mac breathed a sigh of relief. He felt guilty enough without having to listen to Iris's version of things, which he was beginning to realize more and more was totally prejudiced against Rachel. But that was the last thing on his mind at the moment. The real problem was that Rachel had still not regained consciousness and he was getting worried.

Ada was also getting edgy, but she tried her best to conceal it. They couldn't all turn to jelly now, she told herself. Somebody had to be strong and she elected herself. Rachel would have expected that of her.

"Why isn't she coming out of it, Ada?" Mac asked, completely distraught.

"I don't know, Mac. Right now, the important thing is that we all stick together and pray."

Mac nodded his head in agreement. "You know, Iris's mother died in childbirth."

"I never knew that, Mac," Ada replied, genuinely surprised. That accounted for his uncharacteristic lack of composure through this ordeal, Ada told herself. In a crisis, Mac Cory was always everyone's anchor, but this time, he had completely fallen apart.

"That's not going to happen to Rachel," Ada assured him. "The worst is over, I can feel it!"

177

Unfortunately, this time Ada's positive thinking didn't hold her in good stead. Dave called Mac into his office a short time later. His expression was serious and Mac knew immediately that Rachel had taken a turn for the worst.

"She's worse, isn't she?"

"Rachel's not responding very well to the medication." Dave explained. "We can't seem to get her fever down."

"What are you going to do?"

"Well, we'd like to try a fairly new drug, that's why I've asked you in here. In most cases, it's produced dramatic results in a matter of hours. At this point, Mac, we can't wait much longer. Secondary infection is starting to set in."

"Is this drug dangerous?"

"As I said, it is new. We don't know if it's dangerous, but so far there haven't been any bad side effects reported. At the worst, it won't be effective. We really don't have a whole lot of options, here. Rachel's resistence is getting lower."

Mac shook his head. "Do whatever you have to, Dave, just get Rachel well."

"If only she'd come to the hospital a little sooner," Dave said. "All of this could have been avoided."

Mac felt his heart sink. "It's all my fault," he murmured.

As Dave had predicted, the drug produced dramatic effects. Rachel's fever began to go down almost immediately. Mac wasn't taking any chances though. He refused to leave his wife's bedside until she woke up. Toward evening, she began to stir and call out his name.

"Mac . . ."

"I'm here, darling," he said, immediately alert.

Rachel's eyes opened. "Where are you, Mac?"

"I'm here, Rachel," he repeated softly.

"Please come home, Mac. I feel so sick . . ."

"Rachel? It's okay, darling." But he realized that she had already drifted back to sleep. Mac felt worse than he ever remembered feeling. Obviously Rachel had called out for him when she began to feel ill, and he was over at Iris's!

"Damn!" he said half aloud. How would Rachel ever be able to forgive him? After all, he was only supposed to have stayed to Iris's for cocktails, and he'd wound up there for half the night! But again he wondered why she hadn't tried to reach him when she'd begun to feel so ill. There had to be some explanation and by God, he was going to get it!

Iris, meanwhile, was pacing nervously around her house while Tracey tried to read a travel magazine. "Why doesn't Daddy call?" she asked, half-rhetorically.

"I'm sure he would have if there had been any change," her friend offered.

"Maybe he knows."

"If that were the case, I'm sure you would have heard."

Iris thought about it a moment and then rushed over to Tracey, pulling her out of the chair. "Come on. We're going to the hospital!"

"But I thought you said Mac wanted you to stay away?"

"Yes, but he wouldn't dare yell at me with you standing there," she reasoned.

"Oh no, Iris. I don't want to get into this any deeper than I already am!" Tracey protested. But with Iris, protests were completely useless.

An hour later, the two women showed up at the hospital. Mac shot his daughter an angry look.

"Tracey was so worried about you, Daddy. I simply had to take her here to show her you were all right."

If she could have, Tracey would have slapped Iris right across the face. This was the second time Iris had used her as a smoke screen, and she was just about sick and tired of the whole thing.

"Actually, I told Iris that you would have called if there was any change," Tracey said, looking her friend in the eye. "Is Rachel any better, Mac?"

"I'm happy to say she's coming around. Of course, she's still a bit delirious. She keeps muttering things in her sleep."

Iris did her best not to show the slightest reaction, but this was worse than she'd imagined. Rachel had already begun to spill the beans, she thought. She just wasn't quite coherent enough for Mac to make sense of it. But reason told Iris that it wouldn't be long now before her goose was cooked.

"What kinds of things is Rachel saying?" Iris asked, feigning concern.

"It's hard to make sense out of it. She keeps calling for me to come home. She must have wanted to reach me before she passed out."

Tracey exchanged a look with Iris. Why she had ever accepted her friend's invitation to Bay City, she could not fathom now. She did remember Iris saying something about how it would be fun. Some fun! Right now, Washington, D.C., and even Claude DeWitt were beginning to look good compared to her present situation.

"I don't want you to put me in the middle anymore," Tracey said, pulling Iris aside.

"Tracey, please! You heard Daddy; Rachel's started to talk. I needed some excuse to get to her. Please, you've got to help me . . . for old times' sake!"

Tracey hated it when Iris put her in these kinds of positions, but impetuous and exasperating as she was most of the time, Iris was still her friend and Tracey did have a strong sense of loyalty. She didn't want to see Iris's relationship with her father ruined, even if she deserved to have that happen—at the very least.

"I don't see what I can possibly do."

"Get Daddy to go down to the cafeteria with you. While you're gone, I'll slip into Rachel's room and have a little chat with her."

"I don't know, Iris. . . ."

"Please, Tracey. You're my only hope."

When she put it that way, there was little Tracey could do but agree. "All right, but this is the *last* time, Iris!"

"I knew I could count on you, darling," Iris said, hugging her friend. Now all they had to do was get Mac downstairs. That proved more difficult than either woman imagined. Finally, Tracey convinced him that he should go outside and at least get some air so he'd look fresh when Rachel woke up.

Seizing her chance, Iris crept down the hallway and stopped outside of Rachel's room. She looked around quickly to make sure she hadn't been followed. Satisfied, she slipped inside. But it soon became apparent that her plan to put the fear of the Lord into Rachel and thereby secure her silence, wasn't going to work. Rachel was in a deep sleep. Iris, however, wasn't giving up quite so easily. Sitting on the bed, she grabbed Rachel's shoulders and started to shake her.

"Wake up, Rachel. I've got to talk to you!" she insisted. "Open your eyes. I know you can hear me. Stop playing these games, or I promise you, you'll regret it."

Just then, the door opened and Russ stood in the entrance. Immediately, he ran to the bed and pulled Iris away.

"What do you think you're doing?" he demanded.

"I just wanted to talk to Rachel," Iris replied innocently.

"I told you once to stay out of here, and I meant it."

"Iris? What the hell are you doing in here?" came Mac's angry whisper as he barreled inside.

"Why is everyone picking on me? I only wanted to see Rachel!"

Russ ushered them all outside. "I won't have yo upsetting her," he insisted.

Mac laid into his daughter. "I told you I didn't want you to come back here—ever!"

"But, Daddy, I couldn't refuse Tracey."

"This has nothing to do with her and you know it!"

"Well, I still don't see what I did that was so wrong. I mean, what was I supposed to do while you and Tracey went off to God knows where?"

Mac narrowed his eyes. This time Iris had really gone too far. "I won't even dignify that with an answer," he bellowed, grabbing her arm and dragging her down the hall. "If I see your face here again, I'll have security throw you out!"

Iris stood with her mouth half-open in amazement as Mac went back into Rachel's room. No matter what he said, she had to get to that woman before she turned Mac against Iris forever. Quietly, she stole down the hallway and waited outside the door, which was slightly ajar.

Rachel had just regained consciousness. *Obviously she's been faking it all along,* Iris thought.

"What happened, Mac?" Rachel asked, confused.

"You collapsed, darling," Mac said tenderly.

Rachel tried to focus. "I remember, I had a terrible pain . . ."

Outside, Iris held her breath. Any minute now, the little witch could ruin her for good.

"Try not to think about it, Rachel," Mac said comfortingly. "The important thing is that you're getting well."

"What about the baby?"

This was the moment Mac had been dreading as he'd watched his wife in her peaceful, oblivious sleep.

"Dave and Russ had to operate," he began slowly.

"The baby, Mac? Did something happen to the baby?" Her tone was panicky, and Mac knew she was not going to handle it well. But he also had to tell her the truth.

"I'm sorry, darling. They couldn't save him. . . ."

"Him?"

"It was a boy, Rachel."

Rachel covered her mouth with her hands. A wild,

frightened look came into her eyes. "No . . . no . . . no!" she repeated, pathetically. Mac tried to calm her, but it was useless as she began to scream uncontrollably. Immediately, Iris ducked into an alcove as Dave raced in with a nurse.

"What happened?" he asked Mac, as he readied a syringe.

"You can't have my baby! No! Please, give me my baby!" Rachel yelled as Dave injected her with a tranquilizer. Within seconds, Rachel fell back on the pillow, tossing fittfully as she slumped into a disturbed sleep.

"I was afraid this would happen," Mac said, bearing the burden of guilt for their loss.

"It'll take time, Mac, but Rachel will come around. It's just a shock to her right now. That's to be expected."

After Dave left, Mac stayed at his wife's bedside, watching her toss and turn.

"Iris . . ." she began to moan. Mac looked at Rachel, puzzled. *Why would she call out Iris's name,* he wondered?

"Mac, please come home . . . Iris, please, I need Mac. . . ."

Moments later Mac walked outside, deeply troubled. He saw his daughter still sitting in the waiting room.

"I didn't want to leave without saying good-bye," she lied.

Mac looked at her steadily. Iris suddenly began to panic. "Why are you staring at me like that?"

"Rachel just murmured something in her sleep," he began, not taking his eyes off her.

Iris's throat became parched. "Well, I guess she's still delirious," she offered quickly.

"Rachel was whispering your name."

"Well, that proves she's delirious," she said, trying to make light of it.

"Is there something you're not telling me, Iris?" Mac demanded.

"Of course not, Daddy," Iris replied, forcing a small laugh. "What could I be keeping from you?"

"I don't know, but it better not have anything to do with Rachel," he warned. He headed back toward his wife's room and disappeared inside.

Iris exhaled deeply. That was a close one, she told herself. Now she really had to get to Rachel before it was too late.

Pat was very near the end of her rope. She was getting it from all sides now: Aunt Liz blamed her for not holding her family together; Marianne blamed her for John's leaving; and John blamed her for all of that and more. Despite all her efforts, her husband had flat-out refused to discuss their problems. Pat really didn't know what else to do. She certainly couldn't keep calling Dave, although the only relaxed moments she seemed to have anymore were those she spent talking with her new friend and confidant. It had never occurred to her, at least not consciously, that there was anything more to it than that.

It was getting dark when John walked in unexpectedly. Pat had been trying to read the evening paper, but she'd found herself rereading the same two lines over and over. When she saw her husband, she hardly knew what to say or feel. All that she could think was that at long last they would have a chance to discuss things like adults and get everything out into the open. She couldn't have been more wrong.

"I'm not staying, Pat," John informed her matter-of-factly as he headed up the stairs to their bedroom. She followed him, puzzled.

"I was hoping you'd come to talk things out," she said finally.

John dragged a large suitcase from the closet and hurled it

on top of the bed. He opened his drawers and began emptying them, one at a time, into his suitcase.

"There's nothing to talk about. I told you that!"

Immediately, Pat was seized with a pang of dread. "What are you doing, John?"

"Moving out."

"That's absurd."

John zipped up his suitcase. "I'll send for the rest of my things tomorrow," he explained, heading back down the stairs.

"But, John, this is crazy!" Pat tried to block his path but he walked around her.

"I'll be at the Avery Hotel if you need to reach me." A moment later, he was out the door, leaving Pat standing in the open doorway, speechless. She couldn't believe what was happening; her husband had packed up and left her. Just like that!

Pat was not sure why, but an hour later she was knocking on her husband's hotel room door. No matter what the final outcome of their relationship was, she was not about to let it fizzle out like this.

"You have no right to treat me like this," she cried when John opened the door.

"I think that should be my line," he remarked.

"I'm your wife. We've spent almost twenty years together. Don't you think our relationship deserves better than this?"

"Is that what you thought when you went off to New York with Dave Gilchrist?"

"Is that what this is about? Dave?"

John looked at her squarely. He was putting up a good front, but Pat knew he was trying desperately to hang on to his pride and for that she felt guilty. But that's where the guilt ended. It was time she stopped blaming herself, she reasoned. What had happened was over and done with. No amount of anger or bitterness or crying was going to change anything.

"Dave is only part of the problem," John said at last. "We're the problem, Pat. Our marriage."

"I know we've had our rough times," she began, agreeing with him.

"Come on, Pat, it's been nothing but rough times for us. You never loved me. I was just a substitute for Tom Baxter."

"I was just a kid then, John," Pat protested.

"Maybe, but over the years you've shown me in a hundred different ways how little you cared about our marriage."

Pat began to feel herself getting angry. "That's not true!" she refuted.

"All you wanted out of our marriage was children. You were miserably unhappy until the twins were born, and afterward, you couldn't have cared less about me. Why do you think I buried myself deeper and deeper into my work? It was because I knew I didn't have a loving wife to come home to."

"If that's the way you felt all these years, why didn't you ever say anything?" Pat asked, genuinely shocked.

"I did, Pat. You just never listened."

"This is really ridiculous, John—"

"Is that all I am to you: ridiculous?" John broke in. "Well, I'm not surprised. I guess I've struck out on both accounts. I've been a failure as a husband and a father."

"You've been a wonderful father," Pat countered.

"Is that why my daughter had an abortion without even telling me?"

"I've tried and tried to explain. Marianne's tried. What more do you want from us?"

"There is only one explanation: none of you have any regard for me at all. I have no home, no family anymore. Maybe I never did."

SUSPICIONS

Pat walked out of the Avery Hotel feeling drained. She wasn't sure how much of what John had said was actually true, but she did know that their marriage was over, and now, for the first time since that day she had been aquitted for Tom Baxter's murder, she was truly alone.

Barbara Weaver was in the lobby when she saw Pat walk out the revolving doors. She could tell by the expression on her face that something awful had happened and Barbara's first thoughts were for John.

Hurriedly, she made her way up to his room. John seemed almost happy to see her.

"I brought over some briefs for you," she began guardedly.

"Always the efficient one, aren't you, Barbara?" John remarked.

"If you'd rather that I left . . ."

John took her hand and led her into the room. "I'd much rather you stayed. I could sure use some cheering up."

Barbara took off her coat. She was wearing a close-fitting powder blue sweater dress, and a single strand of pearls. Before leaving her apartment, she had changed at least five times, but she wasn't really sure she looked good until she saw John's reaction.

"You're quite a vision in that outfit," he said softly.

"Thank you," she replied, feeling a bit awkward. "I saw Pat in the lobby."

John looked away. "She never really loved me, you know."

"Oh, John, I'm sure that isn't true," Barbara countered.

John turned and smiled sadly. "When I first met her she was a frightened eighteen-year-old girl. I saved her life, and she thought she loved me. What did she know about love?"

"Maybe nothing, but she obviously grew to love you."

"Pat has never cared about me, Barbara. The only ones

187

who've ever mattered to her were the kids. I've spent almost half my life with a woman who really didn't want to be married—at least not to me. She was even in love with another man when we got married." John sank down onto the sofa.

Barbara's heart ached for him and instinctively she began to blame Pat for his troubles. "I'm so sorry Pat's hurt you like this," she whispered, sitting down next to him. "I know if I were Pat, I'd thank my lucky stars to have found a man like you!"

John looked at her, half flattered, half confused. Immediately, Barbara was embarrassed. John put his arm around her, needing very desperately to hold someone. "I don't know what I'd do without you, Weaver!" he said, only half-teasing.

Barbara looked up into John's dark, troubled eyes. She had dreamed of the moment when he would take her into his arms and swear his undying love. But that was too much to expect. And it was still too soon. Still, deep within herself, Barbara felt sure that Pat Randolph had just changed the entire course of her life. She would have never openly chased after another woman's husband, but now Pat had as much as handed him over to her on a silver platter. For that, Barbara was undyingly grateful. Where Pat had failed, Barbara would succeed gloriously. She would make John forget the day he ever met Pat. She would make him love her as much as she had loved him from the very beginning, that very first day in his office.

"I'll never let anyone hurt you, John. Not ever again," she said, holding him so closely that she could hear his heartbeat mingling with hers, until there were no longer two divided hearts but one, beating stronger and more quickly and more passionately than ever before.

Iris arrived later that evening at the hospital, and seeing that the way was clear, she made her way to Rachel's room.

SUSPICIONS

Slowly, she opened the door and froze instantly as she saw Mac sitting at his wife's bedside with a lovely poinsettia plant in his hands.

"When Alice heard you were in the hospital, she sent this over. I thought you might like to have it here," Mac explained.

Rachel smiled weakly as she took the card and read it:

Life goes on. You have Mac. Nothing else matters.
Love, Alice

Rachel hugged the card to her breast. When Steve died, she had sent Alice a similar message. How strange it was that she and Alice had seemed to find their way to each other through sadness and tragedy. Still, it was a bond and Rachel was thankful for it. She had Mac, and Alice was quite right, that was all that mattered.

"Oh, Mac, I love you so much," Rachel whispered, throwing her arms around his neck.

"Rachel, darling, I was so worried about you. But thank God, you've come back to me! I'll never let you go again!"

"I'm so sorry I lost our baby," she said softly.

"There was nothing you could do, darling. If anyone's to blame, it's me!"

Rachel put her hand over her husband's mouth gently. "This is no time for blame. Let's just put it all behind us. We have each other. That's all that counts."

As they hugged happily, Iris, still listening at the door, breathed a sigh of relief. Rachel hadn't seized the first opportunity to expose her. That could mean only one of two things: either Rachel was really going to put it all behind because it was too painful, or she was going to wait for a better opportunity to let Iris have it. But for today at least, she was off the hook. Tomorrow was another matter.